T0354671

Galaxy Ambassador: The Celestial Pact

Written by Reid Wong

Order this book online at www.trafford.com
or email orders@trafford.com

Most Trafford titles are also available at major online book retailers.

Print information available on the last page.

ISBN: 978-1-4907-5840-4 (sc)
ISBN: 978-1-4907-5841-1 (hc)
ISBN: 978-1-4907-5839-8 (e)

Library of Congress Control Number: 2015905666

All the story characters found in the book are fictional. Names that are similar
or belong to someone else will be coincidental and unintentional.

Because of the dynamic nature of the Internet, any web addresses or links contained in
this book may have changed since publication and may no longer be valid. The views
expressed in this work are solely those of the author and do not necessarily reflect the
views of the publisher, and the publisher hereby disclaims any responsibility for them.

Any people depicted in stock imagery provided by Thinkstock are models,
and such images are being used for illustrative purposes only.
Certain stock imagery © Thinkstock.

Trafford rev. 07/10/2015

 www.trafford.com

North America & international
toll-free: 1 888 232 4444 (USA & Canada)
fax: 812 355 4082

Chapter	Contents	Page No

About the Author

Reid Wong is a first time author attempt at writing this book, all his years he worked for somebody else and still do it today. He put his dreams into reality on this book and he hopes everybody will like his dreams. He is currently working for a second novel of a different category.

Reid Wong Categories of Book

 Military Series

 Science Fiction Series

 Family and friends Series

 Mythology and Ghost series

 Crimes and Suspense

 Tragedy Series

Species Alpo

Species BorboCuli

Species Drometalian

Species Cerotine

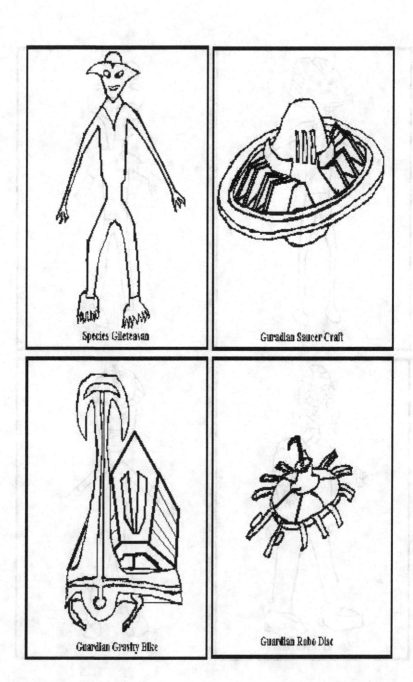

Species Gileteavan

Guradian Saucer Craft

Guardian Gravity Bike

Guardian Robo Disc

Pazarcar Pet Murk Bug

Guardian Console

Species Zarkano

Species Sefornies

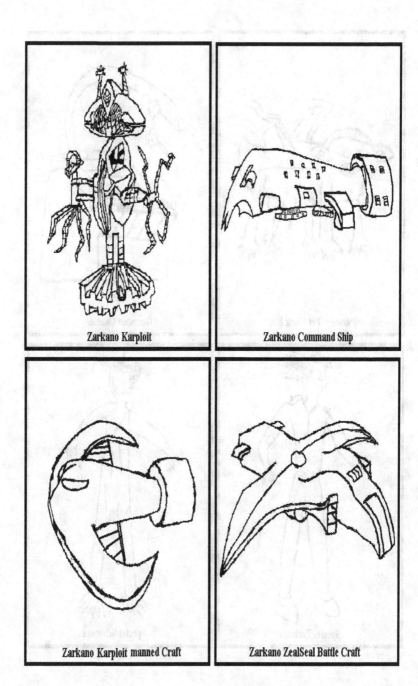

Zarkano Karploit

Zarkano Command Ship

Zarkano Karploit manned Craft

Zarkano ZealSeal Battle Craft

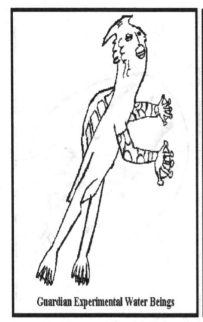

Guardian Experimental Water Beings

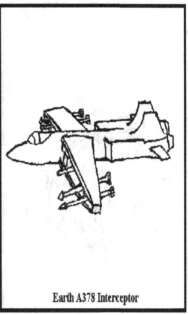

Earth A378 Interceptor

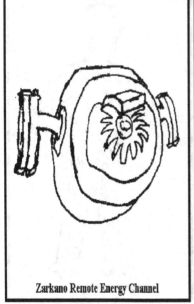

Zarkano Remote Energy Channel

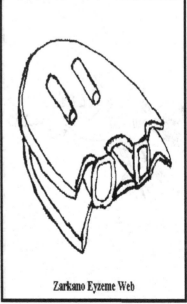

Zarkano Eyzeme Web

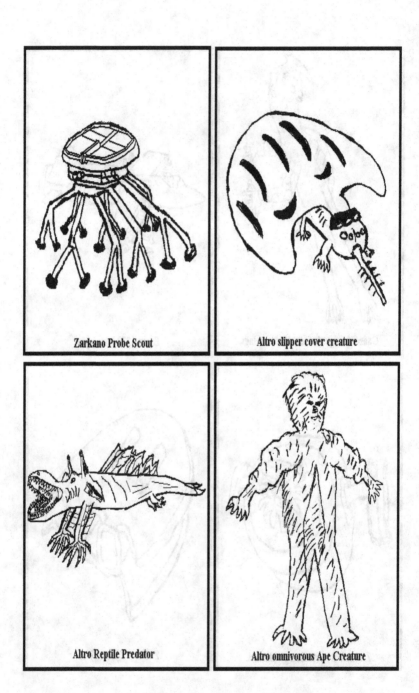

Zarkano Probe Scout

Altro slipper cover creature

Altro Reptile Predator

Altro omnivorous Ape Creature

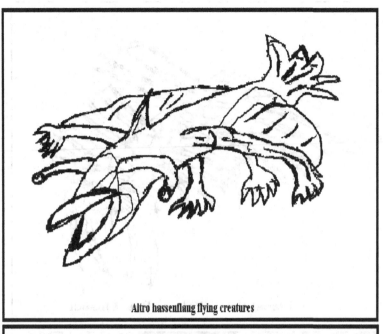

Altro hassenflaug flying creatures

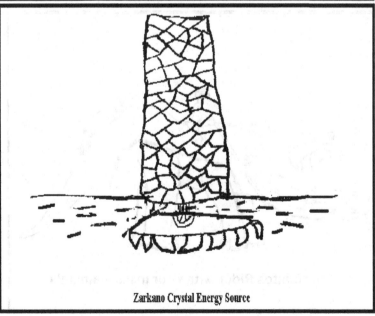

Zarkano Crystal Energy Source

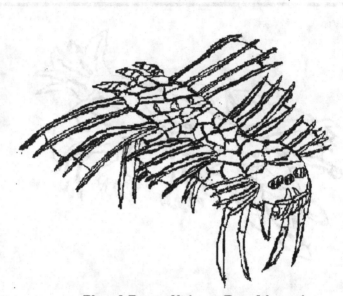

Planet Roxan Yakona Beast Insect

Serfonites Rider with Four tusks mammals

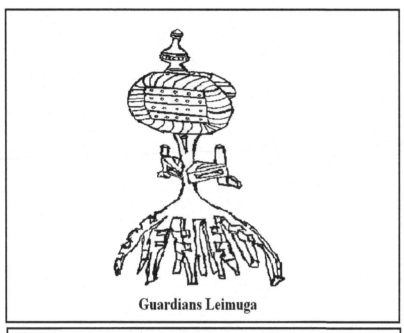

Guardians Leimuga

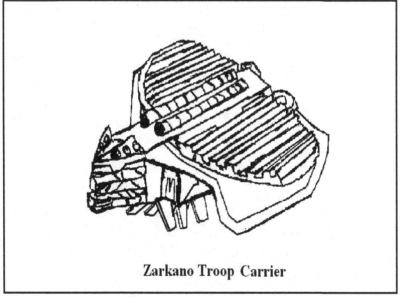

Zarkano Troop Carrier

Notes on Alien Life Forms

It is always thought that humans are the only intelligent life on the galaxy. A fruitless search for living beings in Mars has proven humans are the only intelligent life on planet earth. Yet conspiracies surrounded us when strange flying objects were captured on films and photographs. Verdict: It is left to everybody's mind to believe whether they are hoaxes.

Note: The Picture on the previous pages is to allow the readers to have easier time to imagine the story rather than search the mind to fathom the contents.

Chapter 1

"Always bill, this is always not coming to an end." Maxter lamented as he opens up his envelope and saws bills.

"Son, do not feel dejected, money is the source of human driving force. Take your time". His father commented.

Maxter always loves paranormal subjects. He would frequently read up books and watching documentary on the extra terrestrial information. When his parents have finished watching news, Maxter switched to another channel which was showing "The Bug War". It is a science fiction military movie which depicts the soldiers of the future battle a group of aliens caterpillar bugs.

The show depicts the aliens caterpillar bugs crept out of its hideout and capture a soldier with its claws. Later the caterpillar dismembered the soldier with its massive strength, giving a loud scream.

Then one of the soldiers charged towards the Bug and fired its guns at its upper body. The Bug retaliated and slashed its blade towards the soldiers which amputated him and screamed out loud. The creature scalp could deflect bullets and tries to kill the crippled soldier, but the soldiers shot the mouth which felt hurt and it roared. The soldier creep away in pain and the creature fell on him, killing the soldier. Another worm tries to infiltrate the soldier positions. The soldier grabs his grenade and removes the pin. He was ready to hurl the grenade when another bugs appear from his rear and severed his hand. The grenade explodes disintegrating the bug head and the soldier's body. Maxter enjoyed the movie very much while his mother switches over to a love drama in another channel.

"Mom, what are you doing? There is much excitement on that previous show." Maxter questioned.

"Well son, learn to watch some love stories and court a nice girlfriend. You need to marry one day. Learn to be romantic." Maxter's mother requested.

"Mother, women learned to love what we are and not adore the romantic side. There are divorces and separations every day." Maxter explained.

"Yes it is still better than watching evil creatures and living with such violence acts which are not helping you at all. Look at your strange equipment inside the room, it is taking up space. Those strange glyph on the wall are frightening. It does not serve any purpose at all." Maxter mother shouted.

"Well mother, you do not understand they are great treasures." Maxter replied.

"Well I cannot understand how those junks will look like treasures." Maxter's mother lamented.

"Alright Mum, I will switch over to that channel and let you watch that dull drama." Maxter agreed to his mother's request and trying to switch back to the love drama. He accidentally scroll the channel to a live game show and saw a lady holds a laser ray and pin point a light emitting sensor sensor. The first sensor light up. The bulb is a circle loop. The lady tries to make the bulb light up.

"You must complete the circle loop with laser light, just like in the dark where six people in each building can see the light see towards them." The presenter announced.

Maxter was taken aback as he read a book that a king needs to summon the god by lighting up a fire and descend to five location in the sky, so that the gods can see however the five stars location are not specified.

He then read the aeronautical coordinates of the Egyptian and Mayan pyramid which gave him which gave him the idea that they are connected by stars round the circle.

"The location of the three Egyptian pyramids and the two Mayan pyramid are located in a star point which closely matches the location of the following stars Orion, Sirius and Procyon. The Pyramids are advanced structure that is not possible duplicate by ancient human tools. If the gods saw the fire then they will appear before them. Fire is only invent in the ancient times and it gives out light. However fire is too dim to be seen from the other side. Light produced by electrical spot light can be seen from another person at a longer distance. A powerful spot light will do the trick." Maxter thinks.

Maxter then brought out a large spot light and its supporting stand from his storeroom. He then loads his equipment in his company van. He drove the van into the open field space with no obstruction building and unloads the equipment.

Using the car battery which provides a higher voltage for the lamp, Maxter locates the first star, the Betelgeuse and he shines it he then stretch it across to Merissa followed by Bellatrix, Mintaka, Alnilam, Alintak and finally he maneuvers the spotlight back to Betelgeuse. Maxter rests for a while and wanted to quench his thirst as moving his torch light requires great strength, he then quenched his thirst by drinking his water bottle from his van, he then goes back to his seat. He looks at his watch and it is nine thirty in the evening. Next he gazes at the sky and observed the stars that he point the light source on, suddenly the stars disappear one by one after the completed loop.

"What is going on? The stars are gone." Maxter murmured.

Suddenly the star constellation shoots a beam directly at Maxter. He saw translucent blue beams target on him and he fell down. The torch light suddenly turns off. He was struggling as he saw multiple translucent creatures with sixteen legs creeping aboard him, he try to hit them but it appears like it appears translucent when he slaps the bug on his hand. The bug then enters his body and he felt unconscious.

A while later, Maxter wakes up and finds the time still at 09:30hrs at the night. He felt something has happened, he remembered his torch light was turns off but he found that it has turn on again. He could not remember how he ends up sitting at the open field. Maxter felt some tiredness in moving his arm. He then get up and attempt to repeat the process of using the light to shine on the five stars. The cycle was completed however nothing happens.

Having fruitless success, he hauls the equipment back to his van, however he found his bottle of water is only half filled. He wondered what has happened in the surrounding. He remembers that he never drinks from his water but only half of the bottle is left. Puzzled by such bizarre relief, he headed back home.

The next morning, Maxter was at his desk working again. However he is frowning what has actually happened last night. Meanwhile his subordinate Lex walks towards his working cubicle.

"What are you thinking?" Lex asked.

"Nothing, what are you doing here?" Maxter replied.

"Showing my gratitude for helping me to get my dream girl." Lex answered.

"Helping you? Please kindly elaborate." Maxter asked.

"The term **"Digging the heart for you"** you do remember, that trick works. She was scared when my leg stepped on the air pump which makes the cake moving. Then she was impressed when the small balloon blows out and she saw on the balloon **"I love Gracie"**. Then she confessed to me that it was fun. How you do you get this idea." Maxter laughed.

"From some history books, a noble man was convicted of seducing the king's consort and sentenced to death. While he was on his way to his execution ground, he shouted to the concubine **"My heart goes to you"**. First his limbs and hand were severed, it is followed by the cutting of his heart and displayed to the public. Eventually the severed head are showcased at the gate to instill fear on the masses." Maxter answered.

"Well that is gruesome, but historical lessons promoted our intelligence. Tonight is the annual company dinner, you can't slip it past this year." Lex commented.

"I always hate this day, but I pick the quiz section. It always works well for me." Maxter speaks as he pulled out his ticket for the quiz.

"No more quiz section. I exchanged it with you for this year." Lex took Maxter ticket and changed it with a dance ticket.

"What are you doing?" Maxter hastily asked.

"You are going to dance with Betsy tonight, she have been facing you for six years, give each other a chance. Do not keep yourself on a remote island or be lonely all your life." Lex answered.

"No you can't do this. I will be embarrassed for such event." Maxter said with fear.

"Yes you can, stop thinking about those stupid super soldiers and lethal monsters, you are getting her tonight. Boss is now making an inspection, I need to dismiss myself." Lex commented.

Meanwhile a light suddenly pulled out in the earth orbit, a round spinning object of about forty meters in diameter suddenly appears and flew into air. It then sped across the Atlantic Ocean at a hundred kilometers per hour towards London. It was observed by two American astronauts in the International Space Station who reported the matter to NASA.

"Unidentified Flying Object sighted in space and heading to Earth, kindly notify all nations for preparation against such threats." The astronaut reported.

The day finally turn dawn, Maxter prepares to leave his desk and heads for home to dress well.

Meanwhile at the radar air base, a radar operator spotted an object moving at amazing speed and send out FFI detector. There was no response. He panics and reports to his officer.

"Sir, look a look at this object. It does not respond after we send them a message and they comes from nowhere." The radar operator claimed.

"Any of you notice that object from any direction?" The commander asked.

"Sir, we do not spot anything." The other responded.

"Sir it has arrived at the central area at a very fast speed. The signal appears again." The radar operator commented.

"Locate the last sighted position. Rodney, notify the land forces at once." The commander ordered.

At dawn, Maxter depart his company and headed for home. Lots of people also walking the route as him which will lead to the bus stop. A male passerby saw the sky and saw an Unidentified Flying Object hovering.

"Look, what is that?" The male passer by shouted.

On the saucer, an alien creature named Pazarcar looked at the hologram where he detected the signal energy reading is high on their saucer processing unit which is searching alien's trace material in earth.

"We are approaching our concealing trace substances in this zone." Pazarcar's vice commander Calok reported.

"The trace substance is in that human body. Land our ship and we will approached him." Pazarcar ordered.

The other aliens named Lacus drive down the ship with his mind control and Lacus is preparing connecting a cable like equipment to their sophisticated machinery.

The people screams as the saucer descend down. Maxter and some passerby press forward to see what has happened. Maxter was surprised to find an unidentified craft landing on the soil. The unidentified craft then exhumes out gases from its shutter. Next the shutter rolls down to its plate.

The saucer opens up its metal cockpit and Calok activates the electromagnetic pulse. The passerby takes their cell phone to capture the image but the phones are not working because of electromagnetic interference. Maxter saw three aliens in anti gravity bike appear from the top and head towards him. Pazarcar and his groups moved towards Maxter and spoke to him with a mechanical translator which is attached to the body and it speaks out.

"You are the one whom we are searching for, we mean no harm." Pazarcar reminded.

Maxter watched with curiosity as Pazarcar nostrils glowed when the latter speaks.

"I cannot fathom your explanation? You searching for me, where do you come from?" Maxter asked.

"Eventually you will know the answer." Pazarcar told him as he activated his console on his anti gravity bike which activate a hologram, he touched a panel which draws out some blue translucent bug material from Maxter's body which travels through the ground before being absorbed by a tube on the Pazarcar's bike.

Maxter remembered that he saw such translucent bug before, but he has forgotten the time and venue. Calok studied the planet and solar system characteristics by communicating with its allies, while Lacus analyzed Maxter characteristics, body structures and memory patterns.

"It is a pleasure to meet you. My name is Maxter Anfred. Welcome to Earth." Maxter pleasantly greeted and introduced himself.

"He is curious about us and show interest in outer terrestrial beings." Lacus whispered.

"We will make you our representative on this planet. We arrived in peace." Pazarcar replied.

"I afraid I cannot accomplish this. Maybe you should find our leader on this planet. I will try my best to help you. I can interpret your intentions to our leader for today and show you the place around." Maxter replied.

"We like to go as we please, but we really wanted you to convey our messages throughout our stay on this planet." Pazarcar replied.

"Why me?" Maxter asked.

At this moment, some troops have arrived and assembled. They armed with their guns towards the aliens with infra red spots seen on Pazarcar, Calok and Lacus body.

"Sir, what are they and there is a spaceship. Are they extras in the film set?" Vice Commander asked.

"Our weapons will make them talk." The commander replied as he raised his speaker.

"Whoever you are, raised your hand up and lay down your weapons. We will confiscate your ship." The commander boldly requested.

"I will never entertain such audacity by these humans. Use our shield." Pazarcar ordered.

"Stop it, lower down your weapons, they mean no harm." Maxter shouted.

The visitor's mind abilities could communicate with their console and a shield is activated protecting them. The commander still wanted the visitors to raise their hand up for surrender.

"Sir, they come in peace from outer space. Could you please tell your men to retreat." Maxter pleaded.

"No, what if they fired at us. They have to act in compliant with the law, I forbid it. Soldiers, fire at will." The commander ordered.

The troops fired their shots towards the aliens and it cannot penetrate the aliens shield.

"Those puny human weapons cannot hurt us. Let's show them the cost they have to pay for aggressive action against us." Pazarcar ordered.

The Commander fired his pistol.

Calok activated a flying disc from the saucer which comes out. The aliens start aiming the soldiers' body by sending signals to the disc using mind controls. Maxter is afraid that the aliens would reduce their soldiers bodies to bones and he immediately pushes the commander down.

"Tell your soldiers to drop the weapons, they will not be merciful. No fatalities please. That flying disc could be sort of weapons." Maxter exclaimed.

"No, they must be put down their weapons." The commander replied.

"Do not hurt them, I beg of you." Maxter pleaded the aliens.

The aliens wanted to gain the Maxter's trust. Pazarcar upon seeing Maxter attempting to defend both side changes his mind and ordered Calok and Lacus to neutralize the soldiers' weapon. The two aliens obeyed his command.

"Targeting Done." Lacus asked.

"Exhume the target!" Pazarcar ordered.

The disc fired its multiple beams in a quick stroke towards the soldier arms and the guns flew of its soldiers hand after an explosion inside the guns. There are smokes flow out of the barrel and a tiny size red alien bug was seen out of each guns. The pistol also flew out of the commander's hand. The bug then evaporated and it strike fear into the commander hearts. The machine gun mounted on the personnel carrier was also dismounted and the bugs are seen running around which then evaporates.

One of the soldiers attempt to pick up the rifles and found the trigger stuck.

"Sir, the trigger is stuck. The rifle is inoperative." The soldiers suggested.

"Soldiers, put down your all weapons and move out. Civilian, calm the aliens and seek their intention." The commander ordered.

"He defended us and will definitely make a good representation of us to his humankind." Calok suggested.

"I could not agree more with you, he is suitable." Pazarcar agreed.

Maxter moves himself towards the aliens.

"Which star system did you come from and what is your purpose here?" Maxter asked.

"We come from the planet of Nekoro. I am here to bestow three gifts to the humans on earth. Promise us that you will stay with us and serve our agenda. If you earthlings could compromise our requests, there will be more gift awarded to your human species." Pazarcar said.

"I will try to help you if ever possible provided that you will not enslaved us and turn this place to a furnace." Maxter replied.

"You believe that we will not do that, besides it is ignominious in our actions to provide you aid and then wiping your race on the next moment. It is depreciating our valuable resources without gaining anything." Pazarcar replied.

"All right, I will take you to our leader and let him have a negotiation with you." Maxter agreed.

"Do as you deed fit and do not disappoint us." Pazarcar commented.

Maxter requested the commander to allow the visitors to meet the Prime Minister.

"I have arranged with my commander. The star visitors will see our leader soon." Commander commented.

"So where do we are going now." Maxter asked.

"To the Indoor Stadium, our commander has arranged security and accommodation for them at that venue. They trusted you, you will need to stay with them till the government arranged officials to take over this." The commander suggested.

"Can your troops lead the way?" Maxter asked.

"Sure, you tell them to follow the lead truck." The commander suggested.

"All right, I will tell them." Maxter accepted the requests.

Pazarcar reads Maxter's mind and spoke.

"I will like to see the surroundings that the humans have accomplished on a human made vehicle. Lacus, Calok back to the saucer and follow us." Pazarcar ordered.

"Commander, I have a request. He will like to travel on the truck to examine the earth surroundings." Maxter asked.

"Request granted." The commander replied.

Meanwhile Maxter spoke to Lex that his company dinner feats need to be canceled.

"Maxter, I know this is no illusion and they have arrived. However it is unethical for you to quit this year company dinner again. Betsy will be drowning on her tears." Lex commented.

"Then you better calm her, the call of duty is important." Maxter commented.

Soon Maxter and Pazarcar move to the truck. Pazarcar used his anti gravity scooter to move on towards the truck. The truck moved slowly. Pazarcar saw tall buildings while moving and praise the humans.

"Those buildings and your automated vehicles exemplified the great progress of the humans." Pazarcar praised

"Why have you decided to reveal yourself to us after so many years in obscurity?" Maxter asked.

"Somebody in earth has called for us." Pazarcar answered.

"Who called you? Is it the human transmission message." Maxter asked.

"We will let you know. The human radio transmission is too slow. We read your mind and character. You ought to be firm in the decision for your human race." Pazarcar commented.

"The humans will not agree with me on any decisions. However there is a committee panel which could decide the human destiny. So which star system which you come from and any allies you found on this planet and are they different from you." Maxter asked.

"We come from the Syfelium System., our allies have come to this planet before. But our race embarked this planet for the first time. In our star system, we and our allies were under the organization of the Five Guardians of Formation. Our allies are different race each but our motive are to create intelligent live forms to fill the universe. It was never changed." Pazarcar commented.

"Including creating human, you mean you created us." Maxter asked.

"Yes, the humans are our formation creations and we again altered the human biological genes when the humans arrived here." Pazarcar commented.

"You would treat us as children as we are your creation." Maxter asked.

"Yes, our allies had educated the humans farming and building eons ago. Later we allowed them to evolve in their own belief." Pazarcar suggested.

"What if your creation never heeds your words?" Maxter asked.

"It would be very wise that you will accept our advice and concocted a treaty with us. The human race future could be unpredictable if you do not heed us. We are here to take the humans to a new phase of evolution." Pazarcar asked.

"We already have what we got, except space exploration which the humans consider primitive as I do admit." Maxter answered.

"We will help you with that, but the humans need to develop their insights." Pazarcar replied.

"You have pis-ionic powers which enabled you to know my mind." Maxter commented.

"We will teach your people if you could secure a treaty with us." Pazarcar replied.

Meanwhile Prime Minister Orson has finished meeting with a foreign minister at this office. The Head of Internal Security Head Winston for the State arrived at his office.

"Sir, there is a piece of news that requires to be brought to your attention." Winston opened up the television and the news broadcast the alien arrival.

"At 6:40pm today, a phenomenon event has occurred. A thirty meter diameter spaceship has landed on an open space near a factory and there are visitors coming out from the ships which are not human. We now take you to the venue where one of the visitors was on aboard the truck with a local citizen was traveling towards the destination. So we do see the visitor and there was a disc shape object flying overhead. The security is very stern and there are troops paving way for the visitors earlier. The local human as we are being informed is acting as an interpreter for the visitors. According to the interpreter, we have been informed that the visitors arrived in peace. Our Prime Minister has been informed and he will present a speech in the late evening. The landing sites have also been cordoned off to allow medical examiners to look for traces of malicious bacteria or germs which might have brought in. We now take you to the landing sites to have an interview with an army commander who witnessed the visitors' arrival."

The screen then switched to the army commander being interviewed by a reporter.

"How do you get to know the space visitors has landed here?" The reporter asked.

"Our radar spotted them traveling at an astonishing fast speed and we thought it is a rocket, so we confirm the last location at here and we quickly come with a team here." The army commander replied.

"According to some witness, there has been some confrontation between the visitors and the troops when the former arrived." The reporter asked.

"No, it was nearly a confrontation when our troops put up their rifles but an interpreter informed us that they are friendly, so we immediately put down our arms and welcome the visitor to the truck. We also remind the civilians to avoid using the phone or traditional camera flash lights on them." The army commander reported.

However a civilian rushes out and talk to the reporters.

"He is lying, those creatures completely neutralized our troop weapons and our weapons cannot penetrate their transparent shield object, and there are large amount of discarded bullets shells here. They cannot protect us if these creatures turn hostile. We will be their slaves or doomed." The civilian shouted.

"What you are doing here, Soldiers get him out of here now!" The army commander ordered.

"What transparent shields is he murmuring about?" The reporter asked.

"Here I showed you. It would hit and bounce back." The civilian replied as he tried to pick up a stone.

"Get him out of there." The army commander shouted.

The civilian picked a stone and throw towards the shield, there was reflected sound. The soldiers grabbed the civilians and the army commander pushed the camera from the shield.

The news program was later telecast back to the studio.

"A civilian have been taken into custody for allegation reporting of false information. Nevertheless, the answers finally arrived to many scholars and researchers on whether we are alone in the Universe. The Prime Minister will arrive to meet the visitors after the foreign minister make a trip to greet the visitors. This is Jasmine reports from Europe Global News." The newscaster reported.

"So those aliens finally come to earth with the spaceships, does they have an armed confrontation with our troops as this civilian told." The Prime Minister asked.

"I just receive this news. I am not very sure with the detail, but I will request information from the military." Winston replied.

"Get it done, in addition called the permanent secretary to help me prepare a speech on this alien matters. I will make a trip to the visitors after a meeting with Conglomerate Insurance president regarding health insurance. Those oppositions insists a lower expenses plan on the poor people and I need to convince the Insurance President to reduce the payment for each citizen further. This country is unable to treat millions of sick people." The Prime Minister speaks.

"Sir, we already got enough votes in the parliament to process the bill. Why worried about them?" Winston asked.

"They would make it as a controversial topic during election. I do not want the voters to lose fate in this topic. Now get going. Inform the secretary of the state to prepare me a draft speech regarding this aliens matter so that I can address the nation." The Prime Minister replied.

Winston agreed to the Prime Minister's demand.

Meanwhile Maxter and Pazarcar finally arrived on the outskirts at the indoor stadium where there are full of people getting a glimpse of the alien and the spaceship.

The crowd then moved towards the aliens which the military try to stop them.

"Let's get an autograph from them. The mystery has become a reality." One of the crowd suggested.

"Get away from here." The commander requested.

However the massive crowd and tourists push towards the barricade which puts strain on the police and military. A truck with banners and sign boards for the World Medical Conference traveling on fast speed try to avoid the rush onlookers and skidded. It knocks to an incoming car and both are overturned when the uncontrollable truck pushes the car at a building.

A lot of oil was leaked from the truck. The crowd screams and moves back. There was a man dropped a lighted cigarette ignite the flames when the crowds scattered back.

"A truck will be blown up with human lives inside." Maxter explained.

"Calok, Lacus save those human from those burning vehicle." Pazarcar asked.

Calok and Lacus turn the shuttle towards the burning vehicle and it opened a depth tunnel with two emitting light sources.

"Fire absorber device ready." Lacus commented.

Then two lights beams were shined on the fire which suck up the fire and hit it surface light source but no visible damage was done to the source emitter. This is because the emitting light limits oxygen to a heavy extent.

When the fire has been put off, Lacus increased the strength of the light beam and this time beam began to lift the overturned vehicles upwards. Then the two vehicles are being turn back as the beam seems to contain some bugs creature who pushed it. Then the vehicle is being place back in its standing position.

Then the two drivers were rescued shortly by the police and the ambulance nearby.

"Mother, what is that straight circular ship. I never see it before in Victory over Europe Day." The little girl asked.

"I do not have any answer. It could be some top secret flying machine. I supposed." The mother answered.

"Are they safe now?" Maxter asked.

"There is no flames of explosion and the humans are assumed to be safe. I suppose." Pazarcar suggested.

An officer opened the door and allowed the Pazarcar, Calok and Lacus to the stadium. Meanwhile the foreign minister arrived towards Maxter and Pazarcar.

"Welcome to Earth, any requests from you will be fulfilled at within our capabilities. It is a historic event. Thanks for your companion help in removing the burned truck so that there are no civilians casualties." The foreign minister replied.

"Who is he?" Pazarcar asked Maxter.

"He is our foreign minister. It is similar to an assistant leader on your ruling council in your star system." Maxter speaks.

Pazarcar then nodded his head with the foreign minister without speaking a word.

"What can we do to help you?" The foreign minister asked.

Pazarcar speaks with Maxter that he do not wished to engage conversation with any leaders of the faction

"All right, I will answered him." Maxter answered as he turned his head towards the foreign minister.

"Sir, one of their objectives is to take human beings to a new phase of civilization, which includes space exploration and interaction with new intelligent life forms. Please bear with him Sir, they have one rule and they will only speak to a species leader." Maxter explained.

Next a Romanian diplomat visits Pazarcar and Maxter. He then speaks to the aliens.

"I understand that. Please do inform him that the human beings will try to give full cooperation." The foreign minister answered.

He raised his hand and try to greet the aliens. Meanwhile Calok and Lacus used its anti gravity large pad which is made of liquid shield to move a console controller to the indoor stadium. The crowd watched with awe.

"What is that pad? It is transparent and yet could hold a heavy metallic object." A man asked.

"Some kind of air shield substance that can defy gravity I suppose." Another man answered.

"It is a pleasure that you come to Earth. Please come and explore our country and we can talk how to expand our relation with each other." The Romanian diplomat asked.

Pazarcar and his group considers humans as its slave creation and refused to acknowledge the equality between them. He refused to shake the diplomat hand. However it is also their culture that they avoided skin contact.

"Our culture defines skin contact as sacred. What exactly is a country." Pazarcar asked.

"A country is a faction here. Our planet is divided into many factions." Maxter replied.

"You must always remember that you represented your species and we are not interested in your faction affairs." Pazarcar reminded.

"Sorry sir, they define skin contact as a rude behavior and individual countries are to raise proposals to them through the United Nation because they only wanted to deal with the messenger of one species." Maxter replied

"All right, I will observe your suggestion." The Romanian diplomat answered.

Later the Prime Minister came and offered to shake his hand but is stopped by the foreign minister.

"Sir, they strongly dislike skin contact." The foreign minister explained.

"It is a historical event today as we always remembered. We are very happy to have a peaceful encounter. Welcome to earth, it is my pleasure to let you have the knowledge of our planet and nation." The Prime Minister said.

Maxter immediately introduced the Prime Minister to Pazarcar.

"He is supreme leader of our faction." Maxter answered.

"Can he change or accept decisions for all the human beings in this planet?" Pazarcar asked.

"No, he to consult Three Hundred and seventy four of such leaders in order for plans to executed." Maxter replied.

"It will be a hassle to spoke with more than three hundred leaders. We only got one regulation which we will speak to one human and is you now. Your decisions represents them." Pazarcar speaks to Maxter as he greets the Prime Minister.

"Sir, their motive is to make treaties with earth. But they are confused to who they would communicate with. It would be justifiable that the World government will have a discussion among themselves." Maxter replied.

"I agreed, let the visitors rest. Winston enforced the security and summon this civilian to see me at the office. I need to address the nation and the world as the host nation for the aliens visitation. Inform the reporters." The Prime Minister ordered.

Meanwhile the workers have set covers and put up beds for the three aliens to rest. They also setup television screen for the aliens to watch. Pazarcar requests Maxter to tell him about what the world news are reporting on television.

Meanwhile the Prime Minister holds a conference with reporters on the agenda of the space visitors on earth.

"The world has witnessed a historical event which shows that we are not alone in this Universe. The space visitors landed on this planet at 18:30 hrs at United Kingdom on an open field near an industrial area. The visitors come in peace and we welcomed them with open arms. Our country has withdrawn films that contain anti-aliens theme. According to a civilian messenger, the visitors wanted to coerce a treaty with the humans on earth. This treaty allows humans to evolve towards a new age of civilization. All countries should cast aside their differences and work together for a plan with the visitors. We hope the United Nation officials could arrived at this country as soon as possible to discuss among with all country diplomats regarding their policies with the space visitors." The Prime Minister announced.

The news switch to an earlier video footage of the star visitors who are traveling with Maxter to the indoor stadium and praised the visitors' effort on rescuing a group of people from an exploding truck. Maxter parents saw the news and are surprised.

"What is our Maxter doing with those creatures, will they do harm to him?" Maxter's mother asked.

"No, these creatures are powerful and the government will protect him. What happened to him? I thought that he is supposed to attend his company dinner tonight but end up siting with those creatures." Maxter's father speaks with a dwindled mind.

At the same time, Maxter and Pazarcar watched the other world news of their reaction to the aliens landing and exchanging of treaties. President of Italy appears on the television suggesting that since the visitors have arrived, all the nations should form an Earth Diplomatic Federation which will help to resolve all treaties and policy with other aliens. A diplomat from an oil rich country Qatar mentioned that if the humans started using alien reverse engineered technology to move planes and ships, it could wreck the oil economy and less technological countries found it hard to survive. The United States Government wanted space exploration with the aliens' help to address the overpopulation problem on earth by moving humans to other habitable planets. China suggested with the threats from other universe, their leaders suggested that Taiwan should unite with China as a whole nation. Malaysian government insisted that using large air ship with alien engines to ferry goods rather than ships could cause ship building and port industry to collapse.

An United Nation spokesman proposes that it need more troops for space exploration with the aliens, they also agreed that a newly discovered planets could help reduce environmental issues and disease relating to over population. A Romanian Leader announced that all nations should sent diplomats to communicate with the visitors so that all nations can benefit together.

Pazarcar saw the news and pondered over the human characteristics.

"Humans should stop quarreling among themselves and united for once now."

"They will try to resolve this under a diplomatic term." Maxter answered.

"What is economy, many faction are bringing up this subject." Pazarcar asked.

Maxter pulled out his wallet and shows him a pound note. Meanwhile Calok and Lacus watched news on the human channel and are surprised when they saw violence and bloodshed on Iraq and bloods are seen on the ground. Then the news switch over to an American drone plane firing missiles attacking terrorist insurgents positions on the border of Pakistan.

"A single note like this contains value. It can help you to get a bigger or smaller mass of food. If a human does not have enough of this, they will hurt another human to get more for their needs. How does it work in your planet?" Pazarcar replied.

"Everyone works and shares the resources. The better performers will have more rest. The lesser superior ones will get less rest. Humans are different, they need greed to spur their intelligence and increase their strong will. Do come here tomorrow dawn, we have a lot to teach you about us so that the exchange of gift between us could start soon." Pazarcar requested.

"I will try my best to assist you for world peace. However I am not a member of our faction council and needs approval to speak to you again. However I will try to persuade them to allow me to stay here and learn from you." Maxter replied.

"That is good, we trust you." Pazarcar said.

"Let me turn off the light so that you can rest." Maxter replied.

When Maxter turns off the light, Pazarcar opened a dim violet transparent light which is shaped like a domed shape tree.

"We take a rest like that." Pazarcar replied.

"It is all right, I will go off now, see you tomorrow." Maxter said as he left the stadium.

Calok and Lacus went over to Pazarcar.

"Can he be trusted?" Calok asked.

"The humans are greedy and have unruly behavior, they are seems divided and try to outdo each other. How could we depend on them?" Lacus asked.

"At this moment, they are the only ones who can help us, the other species are too weak. The Zarkano are constantly plotting against us. Our resources are running low and the exquisite fluid are almost depleted. If we used our full resources to create a conflict with the Zarkano, we will be extinct within two thousand earth years. Our hope rests on him." Pazarcar replied.

"Let hope he do not bring us disappointment." Lacus agreed.

Maxter went out of the stadium and he was met by Winston, the head security for the Prime Minister.

"The Prime Minister wants to see you in person." Winston requested.

Maxter respects his wishes and he follows the former to meet the Prime Minister in the Legislative Office.

The Prime Minister asked Maxter to sit on a chair.

"Well young man, it seems that they do trust you. What do you know about them and any ideas surrounding their sudden appearance?" The Prime Minister asked.

"They come here to secure a treaty with the humans. Their allies had visited earth but this species debuts here on the first occasion. It could be their sudden change of leadership among their allies that they decided to reveal themselves to the humans." Maxter replied.

"Allies on earth. Where are they?" The Prime Minister quoted.

"I am uncertain, but it could be the mystery surrounded those fast flying Unidentified Flying Objects or Flying Disc which are frequently spotted on North America and Europe and but many government denied their existence." Maxter suggested.

"Well, you have witnessed our troops being defeated by them, will they enslaved us?" The Prime Minister asked.

"No, they claimed that they and their allies create and alter the human genetic code. Their motto is creating intelligent life forms to fill up the universe with their profound biological engineering. They offered us three wishes that we wanted and when we repay them, there will be more rewards coming for us." Maxter answered.

"What they want from us?" The Prime Minister asked.

"I am not sure at the moment. They told me that humans should not diversify from each other and should get united for once." Maxter answered.

"This is the United Nation is trying to do, but there are too many complication involved." The Prime Minister added.

"Sir, I would like to offer my help and become their messenger for their period of stay. They trusted me and wanted me to stay by their side for the moment. They wanted to train me to get to know them so that to ensure our deals with them could be transacted smoothly." Maxter requested.

"Civilian, these affairs are off limits for you. Till the arrival of United Nation appointed ambassador, my men will deal with them. I do not trust a stranger who might want the gift for himself.You are not invited anymore." Winston commented.

"Well I have no other motives for what you think. My immediate concern will be whether they will experience restlessness with my absence." Maxter answered.

"Winston, stop your harsh remark to this gentleman here. He is trying to help." The Prime Minister requested.

"Sir, he is not in the civil service and he has no diplomatic negotiation experience. What if he accepts a treaty that will bring harm to us humans. Diplomats from other nation would pin the blame on us. Furthermore he cannot dealt with other diplomats who will frequent him on information regarding the star visitors. It is a hassle to leave him here." Winston suggested.

The Prime Minister paused for a moment and finally nodded his head.

"Young man. I have to heed my adviser's advice despite your earnest wishes. Every interaction between you and them affects the world and this country. It is the best that the government service would handle this proceedings and leave you out of such matters as you are not a civil servant. I hope you can understand this. However you will be rewarded for today effort." The Prime Minister commented.

"I understand that, Sir." Maxter lamented.

"Winston, reward him with a five hundred pound cheque. Put the expenses under special services. Johnny please send our guest home." The Prime Minister ordered.

Maxter leaves the office with Johnny a security guard who was dressed in a black suit.

"I will take you home." Johnny commented.

"I am hoping to have more interaction with them more." Maxter commented.

"We will contact you if the world government has made an agreement with them. It is not very wise if you intervened the matter as a normal civilian, the earth people would alienate you." Johnny suggested.

"You are right, I should stay my out of such affairs." Maxter admitted.

"I fear most is that what are we going to give them in return, they have everything we possess." Johnny said.

"Their intention bewildered me alike." Maxter commented.

Maxter finally reaches home. His parents are worried that he might get hurt. However he assured themselves that he is fine and will not be attending the aliens matter. His parents finally felt relieved.

Chapter 2

On that night, he reads up a history of the kings in a book of mythology.

"The gods chose a human king and gave the rights to the latter who will command his man. The king answered to the gods themselves and those who oppose the king were either obliterated by natural disaster or lighting. The gods will not answer to the commoners prayers call. The king's prayer session is followed by light from the sky and words appear on the wall indicating irrigation by cutting off the river through a map during drought and planting vegetables and fruits in higher region could achieve a better food ration. When the king dies, a prayer call is heed again for his son to receive the mandate from Gods."

Maxter suddenly thinks of what happened to at the stadium that the aliens refused to spoke to the ministers and leaders.

"It seems that they used this protocol to address the people of earth through a messenger or king. That means I am treated as a messenger and will not be changed. I hope they can change this practice by now." Maxter commented.

The next day, Winston and his armed associates entered the stadium.

"Now we have collected some information on their life through the informer, now we proceed with caution. The Prime Minister will be visiting them soon, so let's gather our recording devices and we will talk to them about the United Nation." Winston ordered.

Lacus enters the saucer to look for their pet the murk bug in the saucer. He instructed a robotic hose to search for them and trap them with the shield. It finally locate them under a liquid metal plank and trap them.

Meanwhile Calok and Pazarcar look at their communication screen when they receive an incoming transmission from their star system.

The screen displays an alien who have a big head and two smaller eyes, he is wearing a space suit and is a Cerotine.

"Senator Trulog, what it is?" Pazarcar asked.

"The Zarkano had broken the truce on colonizing other planets. They will occupied any planet inevitable and their aggression will consume inferior species lives eventually. They refuse to recognize any treaty pact with the Serfornies. It is believed that they will find an opportunity to seize the planet for themselves. They failed to come with terms with us and threatened action if we interfere in their activities. They demand the secret of our portal from us in exchange for peace." Trulog speaks.

"It is absurd. They will destroy every life whenever they go. Those ungrateful ones become greedy once we teach them the art of space exploration and now they demand secrets of the portal. I thought that with their numerous population, they can contribute to our star system coordination and unity instead they have become menace to our star system." Pazarcar angrily commented.

"Some of our creations are needed that could stop their thirst for conquest. How is the agreement with the humans." Trulog asked.

"I have found a human agent to communicate with us, he is curious about us and will definitely aid us in the pact." Pazarcar replied.

"The humans are confused and wary of themselves. I afraid you will have a hard time coercing pact with them because every agreement concerns their individual faction which they cannot agree among themselves. We will monitor the Zarkano activities and will give direction for the Serfornies to flee through nature." Trulog asked.

"Glad to hear you told me that, we will need to press the humans fast to have an agreement." Pazarcar commented.

Trulog ends the transmission and screen turns blank.

"We must press him for training and subjugate the humans to a pact with us." Pazarcar lamented.

"The humans lack unity and felt distinct among themselves. I am concerned when they go there, will they be fighting among themselves or fighting the Zarkano." Calok suggested.

"I do agree with you but we must give up such tasks to the human or we will be gone in less than two thousand earth years with the final extermination of the Zarkano. The human factor is important to our causes because they needed to fight against the Zarkano however their disunity would reduced the rate of victory over the Zarkano. However that rivalry among themselves would done less hurt to other weakened species. Let hope that humans could do us a favor by convincing his species to unite against the Zarkano when we required them." Pazarcar lamented.

Meanwhile Lacus ride in with the anti gravitational bike together with shielded murk bug. The shield is released and the murk bug went out.

Meanwhile Winston approached Pazarcar and takes out a photograph of the United Nation Alien ambassador called Mr Servivo Kruno from Bulgaria.

"I am representing my country to speak to you regarding the earth extra-terrestrial protocol. Our earth representative will be arriving soon as seen in this photograph. You will negotiate your terms with him and I will provide assistance to him and you whenever you needed." Winston speaks.

Pazarcar refused to speak to him because their protocol was to correspond with a chosen human which is Maxter. He then turns away and released a hologram of Maxter. Winston reluctantly speaks in a sterner manner.

"Space traveler. His presence is unnecessary and our men are much more capable. You have to prepare what you want to negotiate with us humans." Winston requested.

Pazarcar raised his left hand and points to the hologram of Maxter again. Winston gets infuriated and holds his hand.

"Dear space travelers, I will not tolerate your arrogance. He is dispensable. If you not interested in speaking with us, get back to space. We do not need your fancy starships and strange gadgets. We already can travel to space and this place can generate revenue if you can get out of here now." Winston harshly speaks.

Pazarcar is petrified and immediately raised Winston's hand away. The console quickly created a shield which struck Winston hard in the face. The guards quickly pulled out their pistols and while the aliens started to form shields to their body and the guard pistols is unable to penetrate. However the shield is less powerful and it gave a blobbing effect after it hit.

Calok immediately used the murk beam to hit one of the guards to the wall. The men then took cover under the metallic doors which they installed for the visitors last night. Pazarcar used the scanners in his hologram and able to detect the men were hiding behind the walls. He activated the anti gravity scooter with blob shields and it was given direction by Pazarcar to move to the sides of the wall and hit the one of the nearest guard. Another guard evade and shoots at the anti gravity bike but to the shield only showing its blobbing effect. The bike then tries to turn its head back and try to knock the guard again. The guard evades again and hit the wall. One of the guard then moves out of the wall, allowing Pazarcar to hit him with murk beam resulting in unconsciousness. The guard then pushes the cupboard down and tries to contain the bike. At first the guard thought that the bike was not functioning anymore but Pazarcar moved the bike again and it pushed the cupboard which knocks down the guard unconscious.

There are two guards still firing at them. Pazarcar noticed the shield gets weaker because they are not powered up by the starship engine.

"Calok, use our maximum energy from the console and brings them down, these humans need some lessons on manner." Pazarcar requested.

Calok reprogrammed the consoles and allows the aliens to fire electromagnetic pulse from the shield.

"Let's drain them out from their cover. Use the attraction force." Lacus asked.

Pazarcar, Calok and Lacus use their mind and fired the pulse which could attract all metals behind it causing the metal cover to hit another guards off guard and the walls pushed to the guards to the wall knocking him unconscious. One of the guards managed to evade and hide behind wooden chairs debris being caused by the electromagnetic pulse which throws metal pieces towards furniture in full force. Behind the guards was a basketball courts.

The aliens send the shield scooter to knock on the remaining guards, however the guards fired it back. The shield is impenetrable by bullet shots and it knock the guard unconscious. Pazarcar and Lacus continue to fire the electromagnetic pulse towards the guards while Calok fired the murk beam ray from the small enclosed beam which is heating the basketball court.

The splattering sounds have caused one of the female attendant Lina to scream when she is preparing breakfast for the Prime Minister. A pistol dropped by one of the guards is pulled by the electromagnetic beam force smashes the mirror splattering the glass. Lina screamed and turned her head to the other side.

Lacus fired an electromagnetic pulse at the guards with the chairs and tables continue to stack like a hill on the guards corners. Pazarcar continues to fire the electromagnetic pulse which pulls another wall with the beam stays at the guard chairs and the high magnetic force strikes the table chairs and pounced the basketball which accelerates the movement of the basketball clamping down fast. Eventually the top basketball court falls off and collapsed on the guard.

Meanwhile Winston awakens and finds all his men are brought down, he locates his pistol and tries to creep to it. Meanwhile two strange looking creatures with wings and a short body with six legs and claws runs towards the pistol. Winston gazes at the murk bug with unease, one of the murk bug steps on the pistol and uses its hand to lift it but their intelligence is limited and could not raised it. The other murk bug tries to grab it and accidentally set off the trigger, causing a bullet sound. The aliens shut down its shield around its body.

"Where does that sound come from?" The Prime Minister asked.

"It is a gun sound from the inside."Johnny answered.

"Let's found out."The Prime Minister ordered.

The Prime Minister and his guard, Johnny immediately ran to the stadium court and found the guards are lying unconscious. Johnny raised his pistol and aliens started to recharge their shields.

Seeing the aliens recovered their shield in a little moment, he puts Johnny hands down to who holds a pistol and raised his hand up indicating no conflict to be anticipated. The aliens deactivated their shield and activated the hologram of Maxter.

"He is our representative's leader, do not harm him. Let return to our seat. He knows what we want." Pazarcar ordered.

"Winston what is going on and explain to me the mess around here." The Prime Minister asked.

"They refused any conversation with us and insisted that civilian to be on their ears. I insisted that he is prohibited in such affairs. I merely hold his hand and they become aggressive." Winston asked.

"Well just grant them this requests, we should be aware that we cannot afford to offend them. You have witnessed their strength and prowess, and now you can afford to commit such serious blunder. Johnny, get that civilian here." The Prime Minister ordered.

"Sir, you are making a big mistake, that civilian might collaborated with them and betray us. He could have requested them to keep this planet to himself, thus wrecking earth. Besides that he is not qualified." Winston answered.

The Prime Minister does not like his suggestion to be criticized by a non Member of Parliament and he holds him down.

"You brought such a mess here and we will become a laughing stock if the foreign reporters witnessed this incident. Look, I do not want to be a guilty man of human extinction when they turned this planet to ashes. Your stiffness in handling on such matter will doom the human race. Winston, defied my orders again and guarding duty on the remote island will be awarded to you alone. You do not see Lisa and your kids anymore. A last warning. Now clear this place up." The Prime Minister asked.

The Prime Minister pulled Winston up and the guards started to clear the debris.

"Johnny, why are you still standing here? Do you hear my instruction clearly?" The Prime Minister asked.

"Yes Sir," Johnny obeyed his order and left the court.

Meanwhile the two murk bugs climbed over the trolley which have food on the plate. Lina tried to get towards the trolley and she was afraid to move further because the murk bug might get agitated and hurt her.

"Lina, where is my breakfast" The Prime Minister asked as he moved towards her.

"Sir, I afraid they have overtaken your breakfast." Lina replied.

The Prime Minister is curious to see the creatures which he knew belong to the visitors. He is surprised to see the creatures great appetite for earth edible substances.

"Lina, ensure our guests are well fed. Winston get your guys to bring me burgers". The Prime Minister ordered.

While at the same time, Maxter boarded a taxi for work. The taxi driver recognized Maxter was the civilian who accompanied with the aliens to the indoor stadium.

"So you are the alien man, I hear you meet the Prime Minister in person discussing on their plans." The taxi driver asked.

"Everyone gets to meet the Prime Minister. It is nothing unusual." Maxter answered.

"Could you help me something, my son is very exciting of aliens and we cannot see them. As you have been their representative once, could you please sign the book for them." The taxi driver replied.

"As a non civil servant, I am not eligible to meet them in person." Maxter suggested.

"It is a pity. I have no toys to give him as we are cash strapped." The taxi driver replied.

Maxter do not like to disappoint children from poor family as it will leave them in despair.

"All right, I will sign it." Maxter answered as he made an autograph on the book.

However the military is still guarding the entrance that the queue goes so long and the traffic becomes stagnant.

"Get me off at the bus stop." Maxter asked.

The taxi driver agreed to his requests and Maxter drop off at the bus stop.

Meanwhile Lex gets off the bus and meet Maxter.

"Well Maxter, you stole the limelight yesterday for being the first person in the world to seek acquaintance with the space visitors. But poor Betsy regretted again for missing a dance with you." Lex said.

"Well it does symbolized marriage are unsuitable for me." Maxter saids.

"So you are not participated in those aliens affairs any more. Don't you?" Lex asked.

"Yes, the visitors wanted to teach me about their life. However the Prime Minister told me that as a non government servant, I should stay out of such affair. I do miss them as I can learn from them." Maxter said as he felt sad.

"Do not feed so sad, maybe the Prime Minister is giving Betsy a chance to end her spinsterhood." Lex suggested.

"All right stop talking about her. I wonder what the visitors are doing now." Maxter commented.

Meanwhile Maxter's mobile phone rang and he answered the call.

"Is this Mister Maxter?" Johnny asked

"Yes, who are you." Maxter answered.

"I am Johnny Carlson, the man who escorted you back to your house. We would like you to bring you to the stadium." Johnny answered.

"What is the matter?Does the visitors wanted to see me." Maxter asked.

"Yes, where are you now." Johnny asked again.

"I am at a bus stop near the venue where the visitors land." Maxter answered.

"Stay right there, I will be coming to fetch you." Johnny requested.

Maxter agreed and Lex curiously asked him.

"What is the matter." Lex asked.

"Time to play mediator. The star visitors wanted to see me again." Maxter commented.

"Well I think you have to take emergency leave again for such important tasks." Lex replied.

Finally the limousine with four patrol bikes arrived along the road and it stops in front of Maxter. Johnny then unwinds the window.

"Get in the car, they are nervous to see you." Johnny requested.

"So you can get such a grand party to welcome you." Lex answered.

Maxter opens the door and let himself inside the back seat of the limousine, however Lex also went in the front door which incurred a rage of Johnny.

"What do you think you are doing? I never request your presence inside the car. Now Please excuse yourself now." Johnny requested.

"I am his protege and an invaluable assistant at work. I am joining him." Lex commented.

"There are a lot of high capable individuals who would work along with him well. There wasn't any needs for such a low talent chap like you. Now get out, before I try something nasty." Johnny threatened Lex.

Maxter played the mediator between them.

"Lex, inform the chairman that I will need to obtain urgent leave." Maxter requested.

"All right. I will get out." Lex speaks as he gets out and opened the front door. He later get himself in the limousine. Johnny throws in another rage.

"Scum, better listen up or you will get a hole on your head." Johnny rages his temper.

"Lex, what are you doing again." Maxter asked.

"Maxter, this planet realized they will need you for a long time. I am joining you." Lex replied.

"You did not heed my warnings. This leaves me no choice but to terminate you on charges for obstruction of peace with intention." Johnny requested as he draws out his pistol. Maxter stopped him.

Lex began to feel fear.

"Hold on for a second. I will persuade him." Maxter pleaded.

Johnny's phone rang and it was from the Prime Minister.

"Johnny, I have a conference with the press and foreign reporters. I need him now for some answers with the visitors. Have you received him?" The Prime Minister asked.

"Yes, he is in the car." Johnny answered.

"Now quickly let him attend to the visitors." The Prime Minister ordered.

"The Prime Minister is waiting let's drive." Johnny requested the driver.

Soon the limousine started its engine and heads towards the stadium.

"What has happened actually, I thought that the government officials have negotiated with them." Maxter asked.

"We have some misunderstanding with them. They demand your presence for negotiation." Johnny replied.

"They wanted me for negotiation. So my conclusion is right." Maxter answered.

"What do you mean?" Johnny asked again.

"I read through the ancient Egypt and Mayans tales. It seems that only the king will negotiated with the gods and the god treat him like a messenger and formulating policy with him. The King says that gods descended from the sky. His people were instructed by the King on how to construct buildings who was in turn advised by the gods. The King was protected by the gods if the king subjects rebel against him. In conclusion the gods were in fact the space visitors and they still carried this age old policy with them on a single human communications with them." Maxter commented.

"I finally understands its ancient rendition of the messenger roles. I do advise that you may have to quit or suspend your present profession to accept this post so that this human aliens affair could be managed in a proper manner. The three favors from the visitors are essential to the people of earth." Johnny answered.

"I would like to accept the post but we have to know what is their hidden agenda for the humans and what do we need from them." Maxter suggested.

"That is quite true. This affects the entire human race." Johnny replied.

"Maxter, you request them to build a castle at your favorite location and obtained golds from them then all the women will be flocking to you. When you enjoyed enough, they wanted your body to be sacrificed. It is still worth it." Lex jokingly commented.

"That is a short term gift, not for greater leap for mankind." Maxter commented.

"Doom suggestion could only be produced by scums like him." Johnny lamented.

"That should be your reward for publicity and effort. Will you agreed to that, Maxter?" Lex commented.

"Maybe you should talk less or my gun will help to silence your mouth and I will be very glad to toss your corpse over the bridge." Johnny angrily answered.

Maxter knew that a quarrel will erupted if he does not keep Lex from sprouting insults and persuades the latter to silence himself.

Finally the limousine finally arrives at the indoor stadium where numerous troops and security forces are patrolling the area. The crowd was waiting with sign boards showing some words welcoming the aliens and some youth group demand a photo session with them.

Maxter and Lex arrived to the inner part of the indoor stadium. Finally the Prime Minister finally arrived to meet Maxter.

"You are correct. They wanted you to translate their message to us. I got a conference. I need you some information such as where they come from and how they get here." The Prime Minister requested.

"I will not discredit you and will ensure the future of human kind will be less hazardous. Sir." Maxter commented.

"With me in assisting him, the visitors will not gain advantage over us humans." Lex stood in front.

"Who are you and where are you from?" The Prime Minister asked.

"I am his assistant at work, so when Maxter performed his universal duty of helping mankind, his assistant become the most valuable around him. Our cooperation frequently bring excellent result." Lex commented.

"Sir, do not believe him. He is distorting facts." Johnny whispered.

"Show me what do you mean by a valuable assistant and how you qualify to be his assistant." The Prime Minister asked.

"We can work telepathically which means we knows each other minds. I can brief you a small presentation." Lex replied.

He immediately presents a pair of cotton toys named Timmy and Jojo. The former is a bear and the other is a big bird. He requests Maxter to hold a plastic tree and politely illustrates the theme.

"One morning, Timmy climbs up the tree and the chop a log branch with his axe, the heavy branch fell on Timmy and knock him down. JoJo found him and ask what happened."

"I am hit by that big branch."

"never mind we will work together. I hold the other end with my claws then you push away."

"All right."

"So the next time, when Timmy have successfully cuts the log with JoJo holding the branch allowing Timmy to push away the log thus accomplishing the tasks. The story tells that Timmy needs a good assistant who understand him, just like me knowing Maxter for so many years and under his expectation." Lex explained.

The Prime Minister gives a smile and agreed to Lex suggestion.

"That is not an great explanation but still considered a valid qualification. For the moment, you are given this job till we have capable people to replace you. Hope you two can work telepathically together and not pathetic cooperation which I do not expect." The Prime Minister commented.

"Sir, do not deceived by his silly cotton toy story. His caliber is questionable." Johnny argued.

"Respect my decision, I do not want to incur any mishap again after this morning incident. Remember many reporters from the world are watching us." The Prime Minister turns to Johnny.

"As the visitors only trusted you, we will petition to the UN and give you a post of the intergalactic Ambassador." The Prime Minister requested.

"Thanks sir, not for the moment I still like my old profession." Maxter answered.

"Well it is your decision, but I will advise you to accomplish such significant tasks for mankind as a big favor." The Prime Minister commented.

"Do not reject the Prime Minister favor. You are given an important posts which will create a great humanity future. That misery job in that sloppy company brings you nothing but more misery." Lex suggested.

"Sir, I will not fail you. We must be on the way, I will fetch you the information once we received it." Maxter answered.

Maxter and Lex then goes to the podium of the indoor stadium to meet the aliens.

Pazarcar felt relieved when he saw Maxter.

"Finally you have arrived. We have important lessons to you to learn about us. You brought somebody here." Pazarcar suggested.

"Lex is here to help me which I instruct him for chores. He will only talk when I ordered him. He speaks only to me and nobody else." Maxter answered.

Lex agreed to Maxter's request.

"We have no opposition to your species planning and doctrine affairs. Nevertheless we think he is better than some of your friends who shown us insolence early this day. If any of your friends tried to test our patience again, we will ensure they are vanquished with the air." Pazarcar commented.

"It is a misunderstanding. Perhaps they do not understand some of the protocols between humans and space visitors." Maxter answered.

"I do not wish to dwell on the past. We need you focus on our serious agenda. Let's begin our lesson fast. You will need to know more about us. Come sit on this anti gravity chair." Pazarcar commented as Lacus and Calok began to merge the two seat and form a chair and a back support.

Maxter moved to the seats and Calok activated a robotics arms which clamp on Maxter head.

"What are they trying to do?" Lex asked.

"Stay calmed, they will not hurt me." Maxter answered.

Then the visitors shine a pen like object to Maxter's eye which makes him tired.

"What is that? My head seems dizzy." Maxter asked.

"We have allocated a portion of your brain cells ready to accept knowledge and you do not need exercise your mind to learn them." Pazarcar commented.

"Could it teach a human to operate a space ship in a shorter period instead of training heavily for a long duration?" Maxter asked.

"Yes, now closes your eyes, we will let you see our world." Pazarcar requested.

Maxter closed his ears and on the lights on Maxter head gears lights up. Then the lights turns green, a holograph of images which represents planets and star systems are being screened and moved very fast in frames. Maxter was sound asleep.

About twenty minutes later, the vision of knowledge ends and Maxter finally wakes up in a dizzy manner.

"Lex, the Prime Minister needs this information. Their species is called the Alpo. They are the members of the few advanced species who formed the five guardians of formation. The other races are the Cerotine, BorboCuli, the Drometalian and the Gileteasan. Their star system is thirty nine years away from earth. They created many intelligence species including humans. Their motto is to create species and put them on different planets, it has depleted their resources since. Could you remember that?" Maxter whispered.

"Too much, the question on how they come here. I need that." Lex asked.

"Yes, they come here through a portal that surpasses time and gravity. They have created portals through their intelligence space light. Their star systems have much more intelligence species than our star systems. There are nine thousands planets in their star systems which human can survive in and their climate, atmospheric pressure which resemblances earth in every manners. Their star system is thirty nine light years from us." Maxter answered.

"I will fetch this information to the aide of the prime ministers" Lex replied.

At this time, the news of the space visitors in the United Kingdom has gained a lot of science fiction fanatics attention in which they visit the country in packs. Meanwhile foreign officials from other countries are flocking to the United Kingdom to hoping to get truce from the space visitors.

Lex fetches the information to Winston, who arranged a proper statement to the prime minister.

Meanwhile the Prime Minister proudly delivered a speech at the conference.

"It is my honor to address everybody in the world for the first time. We have the first information about our space visitors from our messenger. We find out that they come from a planet called Nekoro from the Star System of Syfelium which is thirty nine light years from our planet. Our most advanced rockets would need one million years to reach their destination and fuel limit further handicapped this operation. Their star system contains thousands of habitable planets which are suitable for the humans. The visitors and another four advanced species were the creators of many species in their star system. Our earth scientist have examined and verified other planets in the solar system are deemed inhabitant. The visitors come here through a portal which surpasses time and gravity in just minutes. Earth is very pleased to welcome this visitors and it provides this planet with new challenges and opportunities ahead, this will bring humans to the new level of an unlimited commercial and exploration demographic. I hoped those nations at conflict will end the hostilities,unite for once and brace ourselves for a new beginning. For now, the humans must start learning from the space visitors." The Prime Minister announced.

"What if the visitors turn aggressive and enslaved us." A reporter asked.

"No, because they save some human beings from an accident yesterday. According to sources, they wanted to seek a truce pact with the humans on earth. Our messenger needs to acquire more information. The space visitors have a policy that they wanted only a human to communicate with them. So we have to restrain foreign diplomats from interacting with them." The Prime Minister replied.

"We hope some countries do not keep them to themselves." An Austrian diplomat proposed.

"Mr Schuster, we will not announce their existence to everybody in this planet if we wanted to keep them for ourselves. Kindly observe your eloquence." The Prime Minister commented.

"Sir, will you allow the United Nation diplomats to meet the human messenger." United Nation Permanent Secretary Rafael Juno asked.

"Yes and speaking of this, could Mr Rafael create a post for this human messenger so that it will disseminates individual suspicions that individuals are holding the space visitors for themselves." The Prime Minister requested.

"Yes, we do accept your proposal. We will like to confer him the post of the Galaxy Ambassador, whose tasks is to interact with extra-terrestrial, but I will need to obtain opinion and agreement from the committee panels." Mr Rafael commented.

"Thanks Mister Rafael." The prime minister replied.

Finally Maxter finally wakes up from his near coma.

"So you have finally awakened, you should be able to recall much knowledge on our star system by now as it was embedded in your brain cells. But it will got lost after a long time if you do not learn it again. You have already known to operate our equipment during the sleep learning." Pazarcar asked.

"Yes, I have memory of it. I will show you." Maxter answered.

"Free to display your skills" Pazarcar commented.

Maxter hooked a pipe line antenna and plug to ear and he puts his hand on an identification meter which allows him to point at object in hologram to pick or talk.

He then activated the hologram by pressing the small switch on his hand. A hologram is displayed and he finds the planet Senipro and decided to inspect the surroundings. Maxter noted a humanoid species which is huge and looks like a toad on his head.

"The ChowaRow as described in the memory learning, isn't it?" Maxter asked.

"Yes, they are so slow in learning because of their typical smaller brains but make up for their huge strength. Humans is one of the perfected species that we ever created. If our truce is agreed, the humans have a responsibility of guiding them towards progress." Pazarcar commented.

"Why the humans and not the Guardians Formation?" Maxter asked.

"Our policy is to let our creation co exist peacefully, so the advanced species will render the inferior species assistance." Pazarcar answered.

"How do you examine planet regardless of time and venue, you never established any station on that planet. That non-human beings never notice it." Maxter asked.

"Our sensory device will comes to any portal and travel anywhere at high speed. It is able to prevent collision with its intelligence and it is invisible with their eyes and yours. The surface of these sensory device are made of incredible soft metal." Pazarcar replied.

"It is great. Why are you observing them?" Maxter asked.

"To observe their progress to determine whether it is time to show ourselves to them. Our allies observers frequently saw the human advancement and maybe you may have read about unidentified flying object which are our allies ship." Pazarcar commented.

"So our progress have impressed your formation group." Maxter suggested.

"Yes, your race have taken only seven thousand solar years to achieve a high advancement of knowledge in every area without much aid, which is the most excellent among our creations. So it is time for the human to share responsibilities on the galaxy." Pazarcar commented.

"What responsibility?" Maxter asked.

"Some of your faction puts up peace keeping missions on this planet, but this time round it will be spread to trillion of miles across the universe." Pazarcar commented.

"Only peacekeeping." Maxter asked.

"This is our plans for your race. We will provide some planets with similar temperamental conditions as yours for the human species to begin with. Beware your humans faction will have other agenda for themselves. You should stem them from going on the wrong path. This is not an easy task as you think." Pazarcar replied.

"I understand it, even though our peace keeping mission incurred casualties." Maxter commented.

"You ought to take a rest, because we used plaroinque to induce portion of memory slides to your brain. This substance will form a reactive compound if you utilized your brain cells too much, an earth day of period should dissipate the dizzy syndrome." Pazarcar commented.

"I will follow your advice." Maxter replied.

Chapter 3

Meanwhile in the planet of Roxan, a group of habitual Serfornies are practicing arrow shooting on a corpse of Zarkano envoy Norchis. When an arrow struck the eye of the corpse, the Serfornies celebrated wildly. Meanwhile a large fleet of Zarkano starships appear on the sky with shadow illuminating the Serfornites.

"Deploy our smaller craft to search for them,our Karploits should easily scan for their presence. Aloqi, continue our bombardment from our larger craft till I saw no movement of the those Serfornies on this planet." Zarkano Commander Lorka ordered.

"Yes, Commander they will paid for the loss of envoy Norchis. Our Karploit craft already out in the battlefield." Aloqi obeyed.

Meanwhile a Karploit craft spotted the movement of the Serfornies who used arrows to ambush the Karploit craft but could not pierce the craft armor, the latter turn back and moved forwards. The natives uses a rope trap to hold it but the force by the Karploit craft is too strong and break it. The Karploit craft force pushes back the natives who are trying to stop the former. The natives withdrew to a forested area and the Karploit craft gave chase. One of the Karploit craft finally spotted the natives movement through a scanner and ready maneuver the craft and fired its gun towards them, however it was charged by a large four horns creature being ride by a Serfornies charges from the Karploit side and the latter craft was gored to a large tree, the Karploit craft alarming system flashes on and two piloted Karploits are out of action from the impact. The last Karploits send its last location to the mothership instead of escaping. Next two four tusks creatures crushes the craft from both sides, leaving it aflame with purple smoke. The natives cheered for their victory.

"Sir, we have detected some battles fought in the thick swarm from our Karploits distress signal in that location." Aloqi reported.

"It must be the natives who wanted are trying to take down our fighter craft with limited vision capabilities on a heavily forested sector using ambush with their mass strength. Prepare to demolish that region into ashes." Lorka ordered Aloqi.

Meanwhile Aloqi and his crew turned its mothership's primary guns from the round turret below the ship towards the last distress location and fire its guns. The blast hit the horned creatures and trounced its body thirty meters away leaving it dead. The natives suffer heavy casualties with corpses flying around and more blasts from the large starship result in more casualties. The trees began to crumble and burned, and it exposes a large number of accommodation which the Serfornies lived in.

"A large number of them is hiding there, Aloqi deploy our Zealseal and terminate them." Lorka commanded and Aloqi act on his orders.

The latter begins to send instruction to the Karploit crafts and the manned Zarkno pilots to attack the area.

The Zarkano manned craft is called the ZealSeal which provided more observance as being pilot by a Zarkano beings rather than a controlled Karploit which increase its awareness on intelligence. It carries a more powerful armament and a more robust electro-magnetic shield in additional having superior speed.

"Karploit bots, fetch your findings to me. I will burn this planet till no traces of Serfornies footprint will ever found." The Zarkano pilot ordered.

Soon the remaining natives split their way to flee the battle scene however the Karploits began to chase them with the ZealSeal pilot killing the most of the natives.

"Follow me" a leading Zarkano pilot ordered his contingent of Karploit crafts.

The whole contingent of five ZealSeal and thirty Karploit crafts began to attack the exposed area with superior speed and more natives are killed. The natives follows its leader order began to evacuate the premises. A ZealSeal pilot detects the pilgrims' movement and began to attack. He turns the craft and burst the beam killing some natives and began to give chase. A Serfornites leader oversaw the battle and foresee his species heading towards extermination. He blames himself for his races imminent extinction. He found the vice chief and told the latter about his last resort to stall the enemy and let the others escape.

"The seal off cave on the shrine. I will reach there and move out the stones to release the Yakona, the beast insect. Our great ancestor LeoBaki sacrifices himself at the cave after enduring the pain to allow the beast pierce through his skills. He put leaf in his teeth to stave off the tormenting bite. His perseverance allows his henchmen to have ample time to seal the cave with stones. Find me a four tusks mammals for me to ride and I will thrust the mammal to smash through the caves and let our old foes to deal with our new nemesis. These new enemy are too powerful. Led the children and female folks to the river and submerged when the beasts are released." The village chief ordered.

"It is not possible the beast could dealt with this new threat. Your sacrifice will be in vain." The vice chief asked.

"They are our best solution at the moment. It could form a distraction for our invaders. The beast insect consumed trees with voracious appetite using its fearsome teeth. Let hope it will chew off the enemy material. I wish my sacrifice could be futile to save our people and atone for my incompetency. Shoot a arrow at the shrine when the children and women reaches the shallow water." The chief weeps.

"Do not blame yourself, the Zarkano are too powerful. Let hope the beasts could have breed in multiples during their seclusion in the cave. May our god fully blessed you." The Vice Chief obeyed.

The Yakona is a flying beast insect which possess three wings. Its tenacious one inch curved sharp teeth could tear flesh off of its victim even when they are flying. It was six inches in length and its front foreleg could puncture through soft metal.

The Vice Chief immediately command a henchmen to drop off a four tusks creature which will in turn rode by the chiel. The former bids the chief farewell. The vice chief began to evacuate children and women folk across the river. Meanwhile a child finally found his father who was the Vice Chief in the midst of the battle.

"Why they are killing us, father?" A child asked.

"Garhula, I have no time to explain to you. Race across the river with the children and women folks. It will be a safe passage there. We have an last attempt to deal with them.." The father persuades his child as he ordered a guard to lead the children and women folk towards the river. The Vice chief's child run with the refugees but hide on a rock to wait for his father in middle of the journey.

Meanwhile the Zarkano deployed their land forces from their troop carrier. The Troop carriers could protect the landing troops from ambush with its flap down wings that could deflect projectiles. Three Zarkano leaders with their Karploits fired with their beam gun against the arrow equipped Serfonies who suffered heavy casualties. When the refugees made up of women folk and children finally reached the rivers, the vice chief finally rode the four tusks mammal towards the the river and fired the arrow to signal the chief that the Yakona beasts are ready to ready to release. The Chief immediately rode his four tusks mammal to knock the rocks off. Finally the Yakona insects began to flew in multiples of thousands out of the cave consuming the chief and his four tusks mammals and reducing them to skeletons within a short while.

The Vice Chief ordered his men to race towards the river after burning the forest.

Massive Yakona insects begin their terror and consume wounded Serfornites men in the forest. One of Zarkano ZealSeal craft reported to Lorka that their target was confused by the Yakona's presence which resulted in their image scanner having difficulty in identifying Serfonites movement. Several ZealSeal flew higher to avoid the Yakona, while the many of the Karploit crafts were severely hampered by the Yakona aggression which results in their fuel system being teared off by the beasts lethal teeth.

"Commander, the Serfornites with their last breath have found allies in multiples of flying carnivorous creatures. We have recalled all troop carriers back to our ship to avoid fatalities on our soldiers. Our ZealSeals craft equipped with toxic gas will be ready to spray those creatures to the ground but will hampered our effort in locating those Serfonites." Aloqi says.

"Quickly put those locusts to sleep. Inform the ZealSeals pilots to command the Karploit units and craft out of the forest region. Order the returning ZealSeals to travel over the river by another route without arousing those flying creatures attentions. The Serfonites could be hiding there. " Lorka ordered.

Most of the four tusks mammals are in rampant mood being bitten by the four tusks,and they charged towards the Serfornites causing mass deaths and handicapped those who are not crushed by the animals. Those handicapped Serfonites are later consumed by the masses of Yakona. The Vice chief finally find the women and children and command them to submerge themselves when the Yakona flew over on a occasion. He desperately searched for his son but to avail. He quickly run back and look for him. Five ZealSeal pilots armed with toxic gas tank spray at the mass of Yakona beasts, the plan works and most of the Yakona flees or perished after consuming the toxic air elements.

Meanwhile Garhula spots a four tusks mammal in a burrow ground after two Yakona biting its upper body and on its front right leg. The mammal was struggling to get up but fail ultimately. He pick a palm size stone then immediately run out of his cover and made a jump and kill a Yakona on the leg of the bitten four tusks mammal with his stone. He later proceed to clobber the other Yakona on the upper body of the four tusks mammal to death. The mammal gets up and Garhula eases his pain with mud. He then rides the mammal. Meanwhile eight Karploit crafts are lining out the forest and they killed the Serfornites running out from a flank position. The bodies piled up.

Garhula saw the Karploit crafts are in line and without the enemy noticing. He rodes the four tusks beast rapidly towards the side of the first Karploit craft smash it over the air, the last Karploit craft on the line accidentally hit fallen Karploit craft and destroy it. The Karploit craft scans a large mammal charge through the line and turn the craft sideways. Unfortunately its sight was hidden by the other Karploit craft who rolled over after charge by the mammal. Before the craft could fire, the mammal smash through the windscreen with its horn and deactivated the Karploits inside.

The Serfornies vice chief saw the entire scene and quickly ran over to his son. The Serfonies celebrated a short lived Garhula victory.

The joy turns to sober as the ZealSeals craft starts firing its weapons from the top and many Serfornies are killed, the four tusks mammals was left dead and Garhula is bounced off the his riders seat injuring his leg. The Vice chief helped his son towards the river but they are realized they are surrounded by many Zarkano crafts with its frontal weapon pointing towards them.

The leading Zarkano pilot moves nearer towards the vice chief and his son at fifty meters.

"Those two natives would not escape this calamity." The ZealSeal pilot commented and gave chase.

"Father, I should have listened to you to run across the rivers. I have implicated you." The child said as he weeps.

"Son, you have made me proud. Many Serfonites lived for another day because of your chivalrous action. These ruthless enemy have no means to let us live. We shall watch them from above to witness their retribution." His father replied as he hugged his son.

The ZealSeal pilot finally smiled and fired his shot towards the Serfonies father and child. However a saucer appears at this time who cloaked themselves and the beam was ricocheted by their electromagnetic shield and struck a Karploit craft nearby which exploded in mid air.

"Commander, the guardians have arrived." The ZealSeal pilot inform Aloqi.

"Do not agitate them. Grand Fleet Commander Lorka will negotiate with them." Aloqi ordered.

Soon the Grand fleet commander contacted the guardian which are two Alponian named Ankoro and Polexi.

Meanwhile the Garhula and his father swims across the river under the shield protection of the guardians.

"Lorka, we never knew you are going on such extreme measures to terminate the Serfornies to a great extent. We are hoping that you can lead all the other beings towards progressive on these star systems in the near future. We are clearly disappointed." Ankoro commented.

"Senator Ankoro, they disrespect us by killing our envoy Norchis and wrecking our base here. We cannot afford to lose so many envoys for every diplomatic treaty. We thought they will learn to shown us courtesy after some lessons like this." Lorka commented.

"These natives could not match your weaponry prowess. Your race have never entered a negotiation which benefit them. These people lived by the swarms and they depends on animals to help them. Besides that corpse of envoy Norchis could be a clone and he is hiding somewhere. Sending an incompetent or deranged Norchis for a negotiation which agitated the Serfornies and deliberately started a war with his fake corpse. Your biological clone engineering are progressing fast and orchestrating such a deceptive plan is highly possible. Instead of bringing great hurt to them, you should help them to built their empire and improve their lives by passing them knowledge instead of plundering every available resources for your use." Ankoro suggested.

"Senator Ankoro, our envoy Norchis shows respect towards them. Your idea of the Zarkano masquerading such plot is unfounded. Morever they wanted a good deal at the expense of our huge resources. It will not please the Zarkano empire." Lorka replied.

"It will take long for us to uncover the truth when we find the real envoy Norchis. There are other vacant area which you can explore and collect resources. Such act is intolerable, relinquish your conquest ambition and leave this planet immediately or the guardian formation will end your tyranny here." Ankoro ordered.

Lorka believes that clashing with the guardians will sustain heavy losses and called off the operation immediately.

"Pull us back to space." Lorka ordered.

"Commander, why we have to concede to the guardians demand. We are very near of establishing a colony on this planet without any opposition in the future." Aloqi suggested.

"Compiled to my order." Lorka angrily shouted.

Aloqi obeyed his order and soon the Zarkano fleet retreat with all the smaller craft returning back to the mother ship hanger and moved to the atmosphere.

Ankoro and Polexi also piloted the saucer to the space.

"Let's hope they will not committing another foolish action again." Ankoro commented.

Meanwhile at the starship Vectora, Aloqi meets Lorka.

"Commander, we outnumbered them and we can take them out." Aloqi suggested.

"Patience my friend, our present weapons could not neutralized their shields for now. However we will able to do so in the future. Our weaponry research academy will able to produce wonder weapon that could make the Guardians begged for mercy." Lorka answered.

"Is that so?" Aloqi questioned.

A soldier interrupts the conversation.

"Verqis from Legrogr Research Academy have requested a meeting with you, Commander."

"Bring him to the screen." Lorka ordered.

"Commander Lorka, we have good news for you, we have fully develop a device which could disrupt its energy source that produce the shields." Verqis commented.

Lorka demanded a test. Verqis ordered the bots to lift one radiator object called eyzeme web and he ordered some

Karploits to go inside the ZealSeal craft and energized its shield.

"Now I shall turn on its eyzeme web to low power." Verqis commented.

The shield began to have an effect which seems to entering the craft surface, soon the shields is gone and the bots reported that the shield generator needs time to cool off.

"Excellent, now I want to see results with a higher energy output." Lorka suggested.

The ZealSeal craft energized its shield and the radiator began to emit its energy disrupt and this time a burst sound is heard when the shields causes a negative reaction and bringing its power source in the craft to a standstill and the ZealSeal craft falls down.

"Great, but the guardians shield is more powerful than us." Lorka commented.

"Do not worry, we found out that with more radiators emitting on the shields, the hastier the shields were gone and its radiator disruption causes a compound reaction which absorbs it and nullify the energy source." Verqis commented.

"Get your subordinates ready with the radiator. We will come and fetch them." Lorka requested.

"Yes Commander Lorka." Verqis obeys.

"Aloqi, devise a plan to find a guardian bait. We needed to test the radiator." Lorka ordered.

Aloqi obeyed his command.

Meanwhile back at earth, Maxter visits the aliens again on the next day. He saw the Pazarcar and his assistants are performing a bizzare experiment. He saw a transparent globs in the liquid tank and saw a two feet size strange creatures wading through water. The creatures have grills in the neck but its has webbed hands and leg. Its ear is big and constantly breathing around. It has no eye lid and its mouth look like a carp.

"Calok, the pebbles. We will test its intelligence." Pazarcar said.

Calock acknowledge and he pressed the console switch and monitored the creature brain waves to the hologram.

"Lacus, gave him the food so that it will have energy to lift the stones." Pazarcar commanded.

Lacus program the robotic tube to inject the liquid called plelonis into the experimented creature's shoulder.

"A plelonis which will increases his energy flow." Lacus commented.

Pazacar acknowledges and Lacus put in the plelonis, an inverse star fish object with a head and the creature took it with his hand and swallow it.

The robotic tube then sucked in the pebbles and went over the transparent tank. It then stacks up the pebbles in a legitimate way which looks like a mountain of rocks.

After finishing its meal, the creature turns towards its pebbles and try to pull it away by lifting its hand to push the pebbles.

"He is reacting well to the circumstances by pushing away the stones, but he does not carry its task correctly, he should have use his hand and carry its pebbles." Lacus commented.

"Inject a few notion of consolianite with our probe to raise his intelligence further." Pazarcar ordered.

Then the robotic arm finds the creature and pour small amount of liquid in his head, the creature has a relapse after absorbing the liquid but recover soon, then he started to carry the pebbles away towards the empty area.

"What is that, it is beautiful?" Maxter interrupted.

"A new life which supposed to be bred in water. He will have intelligence and able to lead his own group of species. He is still under experimentation and we need to observe whether he fulfills our requirement." Pazarcar replied.

The creature then learns to push the pebbles towards causing it to drop, but from a mountain it forms a hill.

"Now let's try his intelligence if he could find an easier way to his route." Pazarcar requested.

"We will show a hologram of he trying to cross the hill of pebbles on land, he should have enough breathing air to last for a long time on a surface which will only took a few Lacquer." Calok replied.

Lacus then reprogrammed the hologram and shown the creature crossing the hill but the creature do not understand and fear the hologram thus moving it away from it. Pazarcar determined that the creature lacks sufficient intelligence for the task and called the robotics arms to pull out a celestial tube and its head of the handle turn to show the creature direction. Instead the creature tries to attempt to hide in the rocks.

"He is afraid, perhaps we can called the arm to make him see the instruction on the purported hologram." Lacus suggested.

Calok reprogrammed the arm through his brain wave and the robotic arm chased off the creature from his hiding place but the creature ran circle around the shielded energy tank.

"He lacked the intelligence due to the lack of cembrance cells. Terminate him immediately." Pazarcar ordered.

Calok then programmed the robotic arm which fires a beam that turns the liquid into flammable materials and burns the creature alive.

"We need to inject more cembrance brain cells to add up his intelligence." Pazarcar commented.

"The substance Acqiolostics could only acquired from our star systems. We cannot duplicate the materials here." Lacus suggested.

"Store his biological design, we will further enhance this species when we reached our planet." Pazarcar ordered.

Calok and Lacus programmed more robotic arms to vaccinate the experimental area. Maxter watched the visitors could produced a shield and which absorbs its water and pebbles without any hose, it is just a short contact with the electromagnetic shields, then the robotic tube fired a beam which burns everything dry in the electromagnetic shields.

"It is amazing. But why you have to destroy him." Maxter asked.

"He lacks the intelligence to learn and will behave like ordinary animals. We intend to place him in a liquid filled planet. This new species will need to evolve on its own and defend itself against new threat." Pazarcar replied.

"If we go to their planet then we are a threat to them." Maxter asked again.

"Your race ought to show favor towards them and allow them to benefit, they will in turn help you if you are facing threats. Their evolution will take a very longer time than the humans. I do noticed individual human ambition will certainly hold others back. In order to progress fully, human will have to contend with each other. You must guide them. By the way, what are your plans for your races in our exchange treaty." Pazarcar asked.

"I cannot decide on my own and it concerns the whole human race. I do know that you are not going to destroy us however I will like to know what is the impact for your peace keeping plan for us. Besides I would like to know why the Zarkano race are not fully corporate into the formation and they possessed space flight capability." Maxter curiously asked.

"You are on par with them and definitely I would not want the humans to be second favor towards them. Creators always love their creation and would not let them suffer. However, we need to test the humans on whether they could attained such abilities in guiding others species. Always remembered, the early settlers will reaped more than those who come later. Now tell us how long will you decided with your gift for our treaty." Pazarcar suggested.

"I will try to approach our community of planet deciders again, because every faction has their own opinions and this will bogged down very long even a discussion for one plan." Maxter commented.

"I am not interested in your race proceedings. We are not staying long in this planet so you ought to reach a decision with your fellow humans fast." Pazarcar rebutted.

"I was only a commoner. It will be very tough to make a decision with our leaders." Maxter answered.

"I understand that you willing to help but there are many inexperience with dealing with your leaders. I shall grant you seven earth days to conclude your final decision. Learn our planetary system again and we hope the humans come to a decision." Pazarcar commented.

"It is too short but I shall try to fulfill the humans and your formation treaty. Before I learn the star system again, I shall seek our leader again." Maxter speaks as he walked out.

"I cast my doubt he will not be able to talk his races around." Lacus commented.

"Do we trust the wrong person?" Calok asked.

"We do not have any choices, if we select others it will come out worse that they will create civil war among themselves rather than helping us. He is still the best choice in this planet and he knows that we are not hurting them." Pazarcar suggested.

Calok saw a transmission being sent on a communication screen.

"A transmission." Calock suggested as he returns to view the flat screen again.

It is again Senator Trulog who spoke this time.

"Hail Protector Envoy Pazarcar, we received bad news. The Zarkano refused to ratify any treaties with the primitive Serfornies and invaded the planet leaving horrendous casualties. The latter's resistance is relentless. The Zarkano could have massacred the entire race if not the interference of Senator Ankoro. We will try to negotiate with them and you must try to bring the humans over so that we the creators do not need not to clean up the act of our hostile creation ourselves." Trulog reported.

"Senator Trulog, thanks for the information. I fully agreed that fighting our own creation do hurts and besides our mortal enemies could strike us any moment. We must not let our creations' provocative activities to dispel our focus and plans. The Zarkano are really getting out of hand. I guess we have infuriated them and they will come against us any moment. But the humans are suspicious of themselves. Let hope that human representative will persuade them to help us without prompt." Pazarcar answered.

"The humans wanted to retain their supremacy over each other, the messenger who needs to unite his race together within a short period is implausible. During our tenure as the galaxy protector envoy, some of the powerful faction wanted to retain us and make us signed treaties that benefit their own faction. They cited the reason that their world is not ready yet for our appearance. We are pleased with their decision and keep it to their agreement that we will not appear before their mass crowd. They have explained to their public to deny our existence. It is an irony that they have not resolved their enmities till now." Trulog reported.

"We will not have their way this time around. I will spare no effort to ensure that they are ready to come to our systems with any mishaps." Pazarcrar fumes as he said.

"Senator Pazarcar, we would depend on you." Trulog said as he ended their transmission.

"The Zarkano ultimately show no respect for the guardians formation, their creators. We must press the human representative for a quick decision." Calok asked.

"I agreed but he shows too much passion for his species and the earth faction is too divided for him to decide." Pazarcar replied.

"Give them less rewards should they disagreed and threatened their species with disease from outer space which will falls into this planet." Lacus suggested.

Pazarcar nodded with Lacus suggestion. Pazarcar vowed that he will made Maxter to accommodate his decision when the latter will visits him again.

Meanwhile Maxter heads off to the guards and requested that he meets the Prime Minister. The guards inform the head secretary of Defence Wilson who readily agreed.

The Prime Minister meets Maxter again.

"The star visitors presses the human race for the first agreement of exchange, they refuse to divulge what the humans need to exchange in this treaty. They refused for gold and pure metal for exchange but they would not conduct experiment on humans beings and neither wanted to enslave our planet. They have a slave race called the Zarkano who do not joined the Guardians Formation but possess the ability for space travel. However the visitors wanted us to lead other intelligent species on their star system. I was thinking if the star visitors brought us to their star systems. Would the human started a conflict with the advanced race called Zarkano?" Maxter reported.

"It could be their idea of peacekeeping as their exchange treaty. I have few understanding of their star systems but when it start to concerns this planet sustainability and our species future, it is better that the United Nation decides for themselves. We will respect their decisions." The Prime Minister suggested.

"But what if our country has to send our troops there and got ourselves into war, I could not bear to do that, it will cost thousands of lives lost. The Zarkano is unlike anything we seen in any war." Maxter worried as he speaks.

"There will not be any land occupation without wars in history and it is also unavoidable in this conflict. However we are not hurting our own species which could be our long lost friends and relatives in other countries. This planet is getting more populated and we have not enough space to walk. Growing crops to supply the mass population presents a greater challenge. It is worse in our country with overcrowded cities and limited areas to be expand further. A resettlement could help to cure the over population over the vast land. Humans need to expand their horizon further and therefore sacrifices are necessary." The Prime Minister suggested.

"Well we will hear the planet leaders idealistic views on this matter, though I did not agree violence and death to achieve the necessary objectives." Maxter replied.

"I understand that you feel responsible for the culminating death rate in the future conflict that could be caused by your present action. But do trust me, an early human emigration to the new star system will help to reduce more human casualties in the future. The humans will find living a rapidly overpopulated urbanized planet with scarce food being distributed on individuals. Most government will act on curbing the population. The inhabitable planets around us could not support food production. Thus it obstructed the humans from attaining its goals to improve themselves." The Prime Minister commented.

"It means that we have to get this done as soon as possible, I need to write you a note of the visitor's intentions so that whoever represents the country need to express their intention." Maxter suggested.

"No, we cannot let our government servants announce the visitors intention because we will be drawn into a controversy topic that our country is intending to hide facts from the whole planet. Will you address this to the United Nation envoy?" The Prime Minister replied.

"Yes, definitely, I would prepare a speech to the envoys. What time could I make the speech, Sir?" Maxter asked.

"In half an hour time where the envoys will assembled for another forum discussion on the star visitor's arrival. I will introduce you to them and let you have the opening speech but you need to dress up in a better suit." The Prime Minister suggested as he found Maxter clothes does not present well in a mass crowd which concerns his country prides.

"Yes I agree." Maxter replied.

"Winston, prepared a suit for him." The Prime Minister ordered.

Later, Maxter was welcomed into the hall of Excellence where he greeted the world United Nation Envoy as accompanied by the Prime Minister. The Prime Minister then walked up the stage and introduced Maxter to the United Nation leaders. Next Maxter speaks to the crowd using the microphone.

"Welcome, world leaders, I introduced myself as Maxter Anfred. For the past few days, the world is packed with frenzy upon the arrival of the star visitors and on such period I have been talking with the star visitors. I declared myself that I am working for the goods of all humanity and not favoring any nations. Today I have an important message that the human race is facing a big dilemma over its future. The star visitors are going to exchange treaty with us. This treaty will brought humanity to a new dimension that is no more restricted to earth but to a vast new galaxy. It is a world that no man have gone. The humans will spread their influence over other less superior races thus gaining allies over there." Maxter announced.

"Yes, interpreter. It is seem to be a good deal. What does the star visitors wanted anything from us, they do not need our lesser sophisticated equipment." Belgian UN representative asked.

The diplomats were in awe and speaks among themselves upon hearing this.

"Before I gives the reason, I will like to introduce their world from their study unit which they brought along with their shuttle." Maxter announced.

Maxter introduced a slide show on the television screen who showed the species that the star visitors created and he also showed the solar system in which the star visitor resides.

Finally Maxter shows the image of the Zarkano and their biological data.

"This is the group that we found that the most advanced species in their galaxy which are created by the guardians. They received aid from the guardians in the past and could capable of planetary travel. Earthling will come in contact with them and we might be disrupting their ambition if we ever reached the star system." Maxter asked.

"Interpreter, do you means that the star visitors is trying to bring war to the humans to another group of their own creation when our troops reach there. This is unacceptable because we have never knew their strength and capabilities." A Turkish diplomat asked.

"The human must advance its ideology. In additional, star visitors are rendering us assistance. If we could calm these the star visitors' creation then we can get a good deal out of it. We will have less of the pie if these advanced species travel to more planets uninterrupted. The United Nation shall have the reserved right to decide on the human's future on whether we should grasp the deal." Maxter answered towards the crowd.

"The interpreter has provided a good explanation of the star visitors' agenda. It contains thrills and ills. However we must stop all wars on earth so that the human race could focus on such important tasks." Spanish Diplomat requested.

"Well, thanks for the diplomats reorganization for human future. The star visitors grant us three wishes and they promised us more if the human could perform their capability up to their expectation. My immediate concern at such crucial period is a recommendation of a wish that is to allow the star visitors improve the velocity and fuel efficiency of our existing planes. Oil should still be used till the star visitors were willing to share their knowledge with us on new fuel energy source. However I will allow the consultation panels to decide on my recommendation. " Maxter announced again.

The diplomats chats for a few moments and a representative called Mr Horgon Moore stands up.

"Apparently interpreter, your recommendation provides a solution for a cleaner earth and reduced resource wastage. Well our earth machines must remain distinct from the other species and star visitors could help us with better solution with our future imitation of their advances using reverse engineering." Horgon Moore asked.

"I could not agree more. It concerns earth so we hope the panel to decide without hesitation. The star visitors gave us seven days to conclude our decisions for the three wishes." Maxter replied.

"It is too rush for the whole world to decide, these precious three wishes are grave matters and required a month for all nation to agree upon. Could you help us?" Horgon Moore requested.

"I will try my best to convince them but it may not worked. I will continue to make recommendation plans for the other two wishes which benefits human kind." Maxter answered.

Maxter retreated himself and went down stage. The Prime Minister move up the stage and speak to the diplomats.

"Ladies and gentleman, the interpreter is trying his best to interact around with our new friends and he is trying to helping the humanities. He is the only one chosen to be work with the star visitors. I will beckoned the United Nation council to confer him the title of the Galaxy Ambassador, which means the one to interact with outer beings and let him work comfortably with the role." The Prime Minister requested.

A chant is heard again as the many diplomats are discussing Maxter future.

Finally Mr Hoogan Moore who led the committee panel stood up and speaks to the Prime Minister.

"Mister Prime Minister, we will further discuss on this matter with the committee. It will likely that gentleman would be conferred the title role and it is unpredictable to let the previous alien ambassador to continue his interaction with the visitors. By offending the latter, we could be jeopardizing the future of the human race itself. However it is important that he do not favor any sides in the human faction." Horgan Moore commented.

"We will respect the decision of the committee panels. Meanwhile we need to discuss on an international expedition force that we will sent to their distant star system." The Prime Minister announced.

Maxter moves down the stairs and continues his journey towards the stadium and study the other life forms on the star visitor's star system. Then Lex accompanied him.

"Now that you have risen from unworthy employee in a shabby company to a world indispensable and prominent figure. You do not have to worry about living costs. The world needs you." Lex commented.

"Though I do welcome these star visitors, but I felt that responsibilities fall too much on us. If the cycle do repeat once again, I will evade them. Lex, you must understand our decision costs life which I wanted to avoid."Maxter suggested.

"Somebody have to do the job. It may save more lives in the future as the Prime Minister do explained." Lex replied.

"I do not wish for such trade off when such burden falls on me. But you are correct, the human must take the plunge in order to progress further. So I will patiently wait for the proposal to be executed." Maxter said.

"I understand the United Nation Diplomats might have doubts on your abilities. Do not worry so much? They will not dare to offend the space visitors. I helped you to connect with Betsy tonight." Lex suggested.

"No thanks please. She is very distant to me. I am a man of heavy responsibilities. Do you know that the space visitors will be taking me and the expedition troops to another location ten trillions kilometers from here? The sad news for you and Gracie is that with you as my assistant, you must tag along with me." Maxter fuming as he said.

"Well in this case, I must enjoy my last moment with her. Well I got a questions, will the war between humans itself will end with the arrival of the star visitors." Lex asked.

"I hope so, but this is unlikely as humans are still divided by faction and rivalry existed among them. I do worry that when we are fighting the aggressive species, we are still fighting amongt ourselves. Well we must capture videos of their individual from the hologram." Maxter suggested.

"What capturing those videos again, my hand is almost aching and what could these help further." Lex answered in disparity.

"We must allow the scientist to study the environment around, so that they analyzed the condition for our expedition troops when we reached the destination. There are no available protocol in our electronic equipment that can communicate with the visitors devices, so these is the best method at the moment." Maxter commented.

"All right, looks like I have limited time to spent with Gracie." Lex said.

"Saving the world is more important, Lex." Maxter requested.

Maxter went back to the stadium and approached Pazarcar.

"Our Leaders have been deciding the first exchange between us and your civilization. It would be decided very soon. You should have complete trust in me that humans will fulfill the requests of your civilization once the treaty is acknowledge by both sides. Could I know the disembarkation point at your star systems." Maxter asked.

"The planet Altro will be the passage point for your humans first step into our star systems. Beware of your human intense rivalry which will hurt the universe as well. A united human race will be beneficial." Pazarcar suggested.

"Thanks for your advice. I will ensure the humans stay united in such crisis." Maxter answered.

Maxter then go back to the study console and recall the planet of Altro from his mind, the hologram pops up and he began to study the weather conditions there.

"Lex, record the planet surface and let the astrologists will examine the weather and its humid conditions." Maxter ordered.

On the next day, the Prime Minister visited Maxter and Lex at the Stadium again.

"I have brought you good news. The United Nation committee panel have reached to a verdict to appoint you as the ambassador to the star visitors." The Prime Minister informed Maxter.

"This is indeed great, I wish they could decide quickly on the debut exchanges with the star visitors." Maxter asked.

"There is another good news again. The committee has also accept on your decision on improving the performance of our existing planes using less fuel and increase the speed and stability. We hope that it could be done with their advice but using our earth known resources." The Prime Minister suggested.

"We could uphold our human prides using our invented methods and our own resources. In addition, they might not wanted us know their secrets of their energy systems. I will like to invite them to an air base where they could recommend improvements on our planes structures and engines." Maxter suggested.

"A farsighted idea, Wilson informs the air base commander at the base commander for the arrival of the star visitors and invite the United Nation diplomats to the air base to witness the star visitors recommendation so that they could not accuse us of keeping the star visitors ideas for ourselves." Prime Minister ordered.

"Yes, Sir. I will contact the air base commander immediately and will personally fetch the diplomats to the base." Wilson agreed.

Maxter later departed the room to inform the visitors of the earth deal.

"Pazarcar, our human leaders have to an agreement on the first deal with you which how you will improve our air planes' speed and reduce fuel consumption at the same time. Our human scientist have study the best physics and chemistry but fuel consumption is inhibiting the plane progress. It would be very great if you could offer solution using earth resources to improve." Maxter suggested.

"We have made some studies on the earth substances. We can made recommendation when we inspect your aircraft performance. The human species indeed have a great capabilities to improve themselves rather than depend on others." Pazarcar said as he praised the humans.

"There we will proceed to the air base nearby to see the performance of our aircraft." Maxter replied.

"Take us there so that we can close a deal between the humans and the formation." Pazarcar suggested.

Shortly the star visitors departed through a back door and being boarded by a helicopter together with Maxter and Lex. They finally arrived at the air base at around twenty minutes.

Upon arriving at the air base, Maxter shows the Pazarcar and his assistants the drone jet.

"This is our drone jet and its two jet turbines engines are here. It can cruise over four hundred kilometers at its maximum and it used up the fuel in just one earth hour." Maxter commented.

"Calok, setup the holograph to scan the actual fuel transportation in this plane." Pazarcar ordered.

"I need to reprogrammed the system for the Stature Tube to make an intelligence and its energy flow." Calock said.

"Lacus, help him." Pazarcar ordered.

Calok put his mind to the hologram and everyone was surprised to see the hologram which was constructed with just brain wave.

Later Lacus pulled his hand and put the proposed pin hole metal pieces to the engine thrust.

Calok activate the console and reprogrammed the Starture Tube to allow the tube to gain knowledge of the drone plane structure and its combustion fuselage. Lacus then set up the holograph with the tertian bugs which can withstand immense heat and allowed them to be placed inside the jet engine on a drone plane.

"Our aerial scanners are in place for the observation behavior of the human aerial objects fuel system." Lacus commented.

"Display the plane capabilities." Pazarcar asked.

"Prepare to take flight, commander." Maxter ordered.

"All personnel please clear the flight area for flight launches." A female officer announced on the speaker.

"Preparing to launch five .. four .. three. . two.. one .. zero Ignition started." A recorded speaker announced.

The drone plane ignites its engine and flew out.

Pazarcar, Calok and Lacus sit back and check the holographic fuel flow from the oil source.

"Launch the drones." The commander asked.

Finally Calok and Lacus figure out that the combustion systems lacked fuel for long distance and it is pushing the air resistance causing to increasing the fuel and lowering the velocity.

"Our scanners are able to inspect the fuel structures under extreme heat. Combustion introduced inconsistent oxygen burning, there is a solution using current human engineering which can mix the sulphuric bio-air which can stream its substances into small blobs and scattered its molecules for burning. This process needs metals with lots of pine holes to store it then release the substance with a lever barrel." Calok suggested.

"Yes it can be done to store the smalls for a while and then be pressed to release its energy around slowly with its highest human manufactured quality. This metal must be able to resist heat with the temperature at ten thousand degrees. Spread your thoughts to the hologram so that they can see." Pazarcar suggested.

Next, Pazarcar meet Maxter and gives him the idea.

"A metal piece of such shapes and features needs to be refitted into your plane thrust engines. Let your human excellent makers to reproduce this metal to compress the fires, next add thick oil clusters to this metals which they can turn to bubbles and could add further thrusts." Pazarcar suggested.

"All right, I will translate the ideas to the human scientist and engineers. I would like to present this idea to them using the hologram." Maxter responded.

"Diplomats and scientists, I will explain on this concept proposed by the visitors. They would like us to manufacture such metal of such feature and stitch it into the jet thrust. Next this metal will be programmed to compress the fire with the sulphuric blobs and it is able to dispense it with the same combustion. I understand that it will be laborious to everyone here but for the sake of humanity we need to bring up more ideas immediately." Maxter announced.

"Carbon steels with the alloy 1090 and an additional mild steel surface could resist to high temperature. A redesign is needed" A scientist named Broscui suggested.

"We can supply that." The air force contractor answered.

"How much time it needed to be manufactured and test?" Maxter asked.

"It will take about a week to produce it." The air force contractor announced.

"With additional funds and more assistance provided, could it be done immediately?" Maxter said impatiently.

"I think it can be ready in three days." The air force contractor suggested.

"Make it two, we do not have much time left." Maxter ordered.

"All right, sir. We will show full cooperation with Mr Beluicis." The air force contractor agreed.

Maxter later goes back to greet Pazarcar.

"We need two days to prepare it. Hope you can be patient." Maxter said.

"While this process is still in progress, you could work with your human faction on the second deal with us. Be fast because your race argument will take forever for them to resolve with each other." Pazarcar suggested.

"All right, I will think of solution and proposed to them tomorrow." Maxter replied.

Maxter returns to the diplomat office with Lex for a discussion.

"Lex, I am thinking of a second deal which will be agreed upon by the diplomats and visitors and I have no time to look over inventions by humans. Could you think of some solutions?" Maxter asked.

"Gold or women?" Lex replied.

"Lex, I am unfazed by such ideas. We need knowledge and we cannot find any good use for gold at the moment. Stop mesmerizing the latter idea, you have not lack of those. We are very vulnerable to the people's criticism and you should stop sprouting worthless suggestions which are not mean for mankind. The wishes weigh upon on our shoulders and we have to delivered them flawlessly." Maxter angrily speaks as Lex apologizes over his impractical suggestions.

"What could that be? We already have many electronic devices." Lex answered.

"Then think of what we like most in our life or we like to see." Maxter asked.

Maxter suddenly thinks of his favorite creature in his life is dinosaurs and they were contributed to fossils which becomes crude oil.

"Suddenly I got an idea. Crude oil originate from dinosaurs fossils. We would like the visitors to teach us how to create a large animal like those big dinosaurs with fat meats which breeds fossils. We would rapidly turn them into oil by compressing them into a long depth hole. Fuels will sustain forever." Maxter suggested.

"Well it is an excellent idea, let raise it. The diplomats will likely to listen to you rather than argue among themselves. Alternatively we can suggest events, people that we hated." Lex answered as he paused his mind.

"Nasty people, remember that Alfred which you always shielded me against my work while I am still in training." Lex lamented.

Maxter paused for a moment remembering the first incidents that took place between the soldiers and visitors.

"Shield, the electromagnetic shield. We need their help in this. This would gives our machines great fighting capabilities against the Zarkano and reduce pilot casualties. It would make a good final deal." Maxter suggested.

"It seems difficult to be reverse engineering by humans." Lex answered.

"We will propose it to the United Nation Council." Maxter suggested.

Chapter 4

Meanwhile in the star system of Syfelium, the two Zarkano ZealSeal craft hiding observed a space saucer of the Guardians Formation which belongs to Senator Ankoro is traveling towards the planet of Altro. The two space spacecraft then started to chase after him.

"Commander, we cannot penetrate their shields and we would be hunted down like prey." The pilot suggested.

"Fire at the target, it was our plan." The Zarkano commander Lorka ordered.

The two craft fired the beam towards the saucer which deflected the shields. The alpo ship detected a beam deflection off their shields.

"Zarkano, they are persistent in driving us out of this galaxy, we will capture their crafts and pilots. Then a sanction will be imposed on their ambition. Disengage and head pass the asteroid field " Ankoro ordered the trainee pilot Nicsers.

The two craft disengaged however the Ankoro's ship gave chase. The latter's ship shield could deflect the asteroid sending the asteroids to pieces.

"We will use our light absorber to catch their craft." Polexi suggested and Ankoro agreed.

Soon the saucer gave chase towards the two light space craft in the asteroid field.

"Too many asteroids here to absorb the craft using our weightless beam, we must trap them using our object immune beam." Leader Ankoro suggested.

The Zarkano crafts split ran at high speed to evade capture. Ankoro's ship chases after the Zarkano craft on the left and fired its beam to nearest asteroid. The Zarkano craft dodges the asteroid and turn the craft ninety degrees between towards the two asteroid centers.

"Be careful, they are using the anti movement beam. Turn on the speed object detection scanners." The Zarkano squadron commander advises another.

"We will trap them from the direction of incoming five asteroids simultaneously. Setup the vector maps hologram and release our multiple external projector beams to give better targeting." Ankoro suggested.

Soon the saucer pulled out the projector beam which also possesses shield protector on it. The beam hits three asteroids consecutively which brings about standstill in the object. The craft evade the first asteroid but after turning its radius, it accidentally hits on the second asteroid.

The shields is deactivated and lost control. Meanwhile the Ankoro's saucer is trying to fly ahead of the damaged Zealseal craft but met onslaught large asteroid which affect the movement and communication though the shields is heavily intact.

"We have to wait, the asteroids is hindering our movement." Polexi reported.

The Zarkano pilot maneuver his craft and able to get his shield on. However Ankoro's saucer gains its speed on it and the Zarkano craft is damaging by another asteroid which comes out from slow traveling asteroid. The former detected a large flaming asteroid and launches its projection denotation round substance to slow its movement. Asteroid roaming towards the Zarkano craft and the pilot fires its beam on its forwarding Ankoro's saucer to no effect.

Meanwhile the other Zarkano craft tries to evade asteroid and fires its beam to remove its obstacle. The pilot shot on the asteroids which disperse but hit on the projection detonation which explodes.

"Our guided detonator was gone, but that huge flaming asteroid is still found." The trainee pilot Nicsers explained.

"A large asteriod with such immense weight will shut down our shields." Polexi replied as the ship computer system indicate a red alert.

Meanwhile the damaged craft tries to recharge its energy and fired against the alien craft but to no effect, however it causes disruption to the weakened shield. An asteroid hits again on the shield causing the strength to drop further and shattered the space ship and a probe device drop on the anti gravity system severely, circulate around it and severely disrupting its energy flow to the saucer.

"A shutdown to the power system is necessary if we were to recover the shield to its full power and overcome the defective cycles." Polexi suggested.

"Nicsers, maneuver the ship to that gap could help us recharge our shields." Ankoro ordered.

Then a Zarkano craft still catching them and spring its position towards them despite it hang its ability to dodge the asteroid. Finally the Ankoro observed the explosion below and thought the enemy ship was gone.

"We are safe, lets power down our energy source now and restart to obtain full power." Ankoro suggested.

For a while, the power was down from and a black energy source material turn from red to white and the probe device was picked up the the pipe probe and Polexi commanded the probe to stick it with its anti gravity power which could accumulate energy storage. Then the power was soon restored by Ankoro who pulled the switch. While the shield was energized, the Zarkano craft suddenly appeared from the front.

"We are still a few seconds from full energy in our engine compartment". Polexi lamented.

"This pilot survives the asteroid rampage, we are now taken in, our ship are still vulnerable to be penetrated with their arsenal." Ankoro suggested.

"Now I will get you, superior guardians." The Zarkano pilot said in fury as he struggles to balance his craft and fire the beam.

However a large fireball is illuminating Ankoro craft and the pilot turns craft over. A big asteroid had detonated itself from some distances and its flame spread towards him, Ankoro's saucer eventually power up its shield while the Zarkano craft was swallowed up by the flames of the exploding asteroid.

Finally the whole area of asteroid are being blew off reducing the all the asteroid to pieces. However the shield of Ankoro's ship remained intact. The other Zarkano craft was also damaged from consecutively asteroid explosion that disabled the shield and damaging the rear engine.

When the flames are finally gone, Ankoro and his subordinates finally could see the environments clearly around their ship.

"The asteroids has gone, we can steer through." Ankoro explained.

"Another Zarkano craft seems to be immobilized from our detection device." Polexi remarked as he zooms in the screen.

"Let's capture him for interrogation." Ankoro suggested.

The trainee pilot Nicsers obeyed his command and the saucer race at high velocity to its destination. Finally the Zarkano craft was finally immobilized by Ankoro's saucer beam.

Suddenly a large fleet of Zarkano ship suddenly appears from their invisibility.

"So the smaller craft are the decoy to lure us here. A large amount of Zarkano Fleet, what should we do?" Polexi said in anxiety.

"Although we fall into a ruse. However their most powerful weapons cannot penetrate our shields." Ankoro suggested.

"Prepare to fire the eyzeme web." Lorka ordered.

Soon the beam is fired against the ship. Suddenly the shields shrink itself to Ankoro's ship and cause a brain shock to the crews in the craft, knocking them out and the power was eventually down.

"My Lord, their shields are nullified and their ships comes to a stop. We sent communication signal to the saucer pilots but they have no response." Aloqi rejoiced.

"Capture their ship and try to pry open their cockpit. Once we confront the mass guardians' fleet with our new device. We will be witnessed their extinction soon." Lorka speaks with laughter.

Meanwhile Maxter traveled to the air force base again and oversees the metal fabrication process and the new aircraft structure design with the metal. He consults with a contractor on the progress the wielding process.

"Yes, of course but two days is still needed. I needed to give our workers a period of time to wield the metal to fit the visitors' ideas of a heated compression." The Contractor requested.

On the next day, the air force personnel and Maxter begin to test the jet plane with a newly fitted engine condenser.

"All personnel please proceed to the stands, as we are awaiting the experimental jet prepared to be taken off." An air force officer announced the decision.

"We shall witness the result of an integration of mankind creation with our visitors' contribution advice." Maxter announced.

The female announcer counted from nine to zero and soon the experimental jet took off.

Soon after, all the diplomats and guests arrived at the observation screen. They were surprised that the plane actually flew two times faster than it should be and the remote fuel detection is using only half the fuel than it should be expected, but the plane suddenly dropped from high altitude prompting anguish and worries from the guests.

"It dropped suddenly after attaining the desire height altitude. What happens to it?" Maxter asked.

"Remotely reduce the speed and try to move it upwards. The condenser burns at a fluctuating rates. It causes insufficient air flow sometimes. It needs a much further refined fuel to ensure the lock out of the air transmission." Lacus replied.

Maxter translates the instruction to the officer, who immediately tweak the control.

The jets move it slowly up and able to try upwards after a certain tries.

"We have made it. Let's return the jet to the base and the fuel need to be replaced with a better substance." Maxter suggested.

"We will try it with the diesel fuel when the jet arrived back." The officer replied.

The jet finally arrived back and diesel oil is feed in to the fuel tank. It was tested again and was proven to be able to travel two times faster but only consuming only half of the original storage fuel. The crowds cheers as finally one of the gifts is faithfully delivered.

The next day, Maxter presents himself to the foreign diplomats in the hall.

"The first gift is finally delivered by the visitors. However we have lesser time to decide on the next gift. I would propose the human made energy shields with our visitors' advice. We might encounter deadly species in the other world and so this might help us." Maxter commented.

"I could not agree more with you. All gifts must be made by human invention and our dignity must be preserved." A Hungarian Diplomat Mister David Diplosiki asked.

"Next, the expedition team, I hope our fellow diplomats could send out some of the best soldiers from their respective countries vigorously for this mission. I have evaluated the list of weapons and inventories for the journey. Our tactical commander reckoned that we still need the latest flying armed machine for the showcase of strength." Maxter suggested.

"Ambassador, could I suggest whichever countries sends more troops and equipment for supporting the task force will receive a greater return for their countries." Ukraine Diplomat Sevkopi Polog requested.

"Yes, the rule is base on whoever came out with more manpower and equipment will have a bigger pie among the others. We need planes, armored vehicles, motorized and electronic equipment and men." Maxter agreed.

"The United States will provide the expedition force with its more advanced equipment and tactical groups against the hostile forces." United States Diplomat Larry Horlton suggested.

"We have recommended Commander Tagrin of the US Army 9th Division to be the commander in chief of the expedition force. Let's welcome him to the stage." Maxter announced.

"We will equipped the expedition force with the new A-378 Air Interceptor. It mounted a twin high velocity K-47 tank gun capable of penetrating ten centimeters of steel armor plate at over eight kilometers away. This plane could also accelerate more three thousand two hundred kilometers per hour. The guns barrel could be moved bi-directional and fired at its enemy. Its computer aided firing system could determine the estimated enemy travel location using its velocity from the screen and would guide the fighter pilots to fire at the right time which would hit the target. Two shell will be fired from two twisted angle continuously to score a hit at great accuracy, which results in preserving the plane ammunition from poor aiming control. It could obtain a higher kill ratio with the firing system. Its secondary weapons are four air to air missiles. The main agenda of using high velocity gun is to reduce reliance on missiles which may be exhausted on unprecedented circumstances." Commander Tagrin commented.

"With such great arsenal in our units, I am sure the enemy would not dare to aggravate us. At this moment, we will prefer the individual countries troops rather than the United Nation forces. I hope all nation will immediately made a fast decision regarding troops on this expedition. " Maxter suggested.

The crowd chants and claps their hands.

In the afternoon, Maxter discussed the subjects with Pazarcar on producing a human made energy shields as a second gift.

"The energy shields could be a vital aid to us if we find the Zarkano too hostile. I understand the energy shield might consist of heavy density gases which created its deflection across. There have been rumors that earth scientists attempt to create one but no results have shown that it ever take places. I have brought our best earth chemist along so that we could begin the idea and testing." Maxter said.

"We have acquired information on this planet surrounding surface and atmosphere a long time. But we have not studied it carefully, assuming all life supporting life air will almost be the same. However your chemist could provide us with more information thus saving us the time to make another evaluation." Pazarcar replied.

"This gas Ununoctium has the heaviest density among gases in this planet. But it could be unstable that it might disintegrate and some of this are found in earth most destructive weapons." Maxter answered.

"Then it will be unwise because such gases will dismantled itself and caused the fuels to ignite. So gas should be safe and would not burned when hit but it must be able to crush any objects within the air. It should also be able to bond attraction and keeps it flowing." Pazarcar suggested.

"We do not have knowledge of such gases." Maxter replied.

Pazarcar then showed a hologram towards Maxter.

"It will like serving a combination of different gases. It must be controlled to your will and able to travel at any location protecting the victims. A recommendation of the medium gas will be used and repelling the shrapnel will be useful. Creating a large layer of gases may leads up to heavy fuel usage." Pazarcar suggested.

"In our scientific experiment, metal is more heavy weight than any air and any air is impossible to crush any metal in between." Maxter answered.

"Lacus have developed a formula which could mix the earth substances which could make a shield but your race needs your own determination to make it perfect. You will be able to see the experiment tonight. Developing a shield is not a simple solution with using some equipment to splash around. A mathematical formula is needed which includes the material and substance used to create the compound. This formula will also be given for your human race to achieve perfection upon successful testing." Pazarcar replied.

"I will be happy to see the experiment but I always have some difficulty in understanding complex mathematics from Lacus explanation." Maxter lamented.

"Do not worry, we will convey the formula to convention earth scientists explanation. We began to familiar ourselves with your human scientific domestic protocol. As for the demonstration, could you please get equipment which could absorb air?" Lacus replied.

During the night, Maxter, Lex and three chemists visit Pazarcar and his companions with four vacuum cleaners which Lacus might predicted.

"We have developed an air mixture with the thinnest air density flowing on the outside and a heavier air density on the inside. Now what you would do is that we will release this air and your machines will absorb the air and you will fire your ammunition in this closely gap corner. " Pazarcar requested.

Maxter, together with Lex and the chemist committee switches on the two vacuum cleaners for better and fast absorption of the visitors devised mixture air. Calok upon realizing the vacuum machine has been started then released the mixture air from their small air compressed moveable device which consists of three air tubes.

When the vacuum starts sucking up the air, it clearly forms an air running velvet with the light air forms the top cover layering over the more dense air which is spinning with more speed as it was sucking in by two vacuums.

"I have added a great amount of melted metal which will form metal plates upon heat interaction. Now it gets ready to be tested on." Lacus said.

"Now test the experimental shields with your light ammunition." Pazarcar requested.

Maxter took a gun and fired at the shields. However the shields could be penetrated but the bullets after penetration fell in an awkward manner with the metal cap just losing its sparks.

"Although it penetrated, but it accomplished its shielding purpose with a new concept of blocking capabilities using energy particles." Maxter commented.

"Another fast suction is needed to extinguish its fuels faster and exhausted its trails behind on the second layer of air transition." Lacus suggested.

"Lex, I needed another vacuum is to be placed on the middle section." Maxter said after pausing for a moment.

Lex immediately fetched up another vacuum. The vacuums are placed on the position and Maxter repeated his movement of firing his pistol at the shield. This time, the bullets are block and deflected down.

"It is a successful experimentation. The formula do works. I am really grateful to you. I always thought that those shields which I saw in my own human made program could only be made from substance which is not found in this planet. Are there better substance can be found on other planets that allows the shield to resist heavier projectiles?" Maxter said.

"Yes, Lacus will try to revamp the shield process and will be able to provide a better protection against heavier ammunition. Then the formula will be given it to your human race who will improve on better means." Pazarcar answered.

Maxter left the stadium and he found himself delighted to work with Pazarcar and the visitors. On the next day the Prime Minister and his aides approached Maxter and the latter shows him the video of the reverse engineered electromagnetic shields which is performed last night. The Prime Minister shows extreme satisfaction.

"Thanks Maxter, the earth people should rejoice over the innovation being introduced by the visitors using earth source material. We always believed that we have already reached the limits of our human technical abilities but the visitors have teaches us that we can further utilize our earth resources. However having these two innovations being produced on this soil, it has made this nation proud. It does show our coordination skill even with a stranger is highly admired. You have done remarkably well, young man. Such versatile intellectual skills could made you a outstanding coordinator for your previous company. I suppose" The Prime Minister praises Maxter.

"It is exactly the opposite. I seldom meet clients and an introvert person which explains I am still a bachelor. I studied more prehistoric elements and mysteries which make me easier to communicate with them. Maybe people could coordinated with other beings well better with scheming humans. When I passed on this task to the next ambassador, I would go back where I belong. Public service is not my cup of tea." Maxter explained.

"The human factor is a great depth for understanding. I understand it is a great responsibility for you now. But you will enjoy a great future here." The Prime Minister replied and smiles as he walked away.

"The Prime Minister is correct. Why goes back to that slump area and be a nobody? Your perplexed mind really drive our mind towards bewilderment." Lex replied.

"You should know when the world future rested heavily on your shoulder and a wrongful step will bring your name to shame forever." Maxter answered.

At the auditorium, Maxter is hosting the foreign diplomats and he shows videos of the energy shield made from earth resources with the assistance of the visitors.

"The formula will be given to us soon. Our last wish from the visitors is pending everyone suggestion. It would be great if everybody could fill up the suggestion at this distributed form. Then we will decide for the subject who has raised the highest number of suggestion among us. However I will support the idea of reinvention of fossil fuels with rejuvenation of large animals." Maxter announced.

"We need a greater amount of time to put the last idea to work." A Taiwanese minister Mr Chen Mao Sheng expressed.

"Sorry Mr Chen, this plan must be made known today. There will be an expedition force exploring the star system and we do not know whether the aggressive beings from that star system could reach an agreement with us. So gentleman, please do not hesitant about the proposal requests." Maxter answered.

The diplomats were having discussed with their own countrymen politicians and penned their last wishes to the form. The department of security calculated the suggestion and finally it was submitted to Maxter who announced the decision.

"Now we finally found a conclusion to the most wanted wishes from our visitors. The gift of reinventing of fossil fuels." Maxter announced.

"How do you expect the visitors to help us." Indian Diplomat Dipika Balarkis asked.

"Well dinosaurs meats and bones contribute to fossil fuels, so we do require large mammals for such fuels to supply our machinery. I will need their help to rejuvenate those ancient creatures. So all nations have agreed on this proposal and we will proceed as follow." Maxter replied.

The Prime Minister conveyed his messages to the mass.

"It is a blessing to this planet that the visitors could led us humans to a new era. Now all the wishes have been decided for benefit of all human being. Now I wished to invite everyone of you here for a ceremony which we will be honoring the visitors." Prime Minister answered.

"It is a great pleasure to attend the ceremony and we thanks the Prime Minister for your gracious invitation. We will prepare ourselves for the ceremony." British Diplomat Andrew Parlour commented.

After the crowd has dispersed, the Prime Minister urges Maxter to invite the star visitors for a ceremony at Ringo Square.

"They are least tolerant of camera flashes and high frequency tone. I suppose it was not a good idea." Maxter suggested.

"We have already prohibited reporters from bringing out cameras for photography and our wired microphones are heavily secured." The Prime Minister remarked.

"All right, I will try my best to persuade them." Maxter remarked.

At the stadium Pazarcar and his mates are having a conference with Senator Trulog.

"All hail Galaxy protector envoy Pazarcar. One of the guardians scouts which consists of Senator Ankoro, Polexi and the trainee pilot Nicsers did not reached the desired destination as planned. The last reported location is near a Zarkano occupied air space. We required the presence of the humans in our star system immediately." Trulog explained.

"The Zarkano are out to provoke us for a full scale war. Rest assured we will compelled the humans to do us this favor." Pazarcar suggested.

"Our hope rests on you." Trulog requested as he terminated the transmission.

"There is no time to waste. Those Zarkano scourges would likely to strike against us any moments." Calok suggested.

"They thought we will be very unwilling to lay a touch on them." Lacus angrily commented.

"Yes, we do cherish our creation as much as we do care for ourselves. But we will retaliated with immerse strength if they do go beyond our endurance limits. We must work fast on the humans and our human representative must ensure his race completely aligned to our requests. There will be no time loss for our great plans." Pazarcar commented.

Meanwhile Maxter and Lex reached the stadium again in order to meet the visitors.

"Resurrect those ancient creatures! It means a Jurassic zone in the making. I thought it is always your dream. Well it means no adventurer would ever spend time searching for that Loch Ness." Lex questioned.

"I suppose it is to be. It will be a wonderful return for them into this modern world." Maxter commented

Maxter approached the visitors for the human wish of a third gift.

"Our earth leaders wish to thank you and there will be a ceremony to commemorate your effort for this planet." Maxter requested.

"We are glad to accede to your requests, but we want our treaty pact to be fulfilled immediately. Have you decided for your last wish?" Pazarcar suggested.

"Yes, our planet resources of fuels is running out fast. So we wanted to replenish these fossils by means of the ancient creatures which gave much to these fuels. Only bones were left and we cannot re-clone them as all of the molecular cells have been dried up. Our biological experts have reached a limits of understanding of our own body cells. Could you help us?" Maxter asked.

"We can regenerate the body cells through the bones marrow and its colon ingredients even it has dried up provided it response to our cells brom attraction instruments. We have regenerated its inner cell clots of many beings several times and it will successful cloning this round without doubt." Pazarcar commented.

"Then we would work on existing animals bones them before our ancient huge creatures. Could your biological advance able to replicate a new leg for those humans who have been amputated?" Maxter asked.

"Yes, we have even clone a new leg which could be connected to your veins. Our biological instruments could repair or even reproduced the associate cells for any human beings by using their blood cells." Pazarcar replied.

"Well that is great news for our human soldiers who have lost their limbs in our own war and whom have been frustrated by their cybernetic prosthetic knee. Another question when we have bad cells that occupies our whole body and severely damage every veins, are there any cure for this without dissecting the body?" Maxter asked.

"Yes, the operation will be tedious but an hour of injecting good cells and purging process of the bad cells. Next our probes will form liquid waves that will pull back the damage bones to the actual position and next veins and tissues will grow at accelerating rate to make a human feel afresh." Pazarcar answered.

"It was a fine explanation. Remember that aquatic being which you have experimented on this planet. Would creating a human fish hybrid using humans and aquatic beings produce a more successful experimentation?" Maxter asked.

"It is unfeasible as the human molecular cells will gobbled up the aquatic softer tissues and cells and will form itself as a human again which will drown the species." Pazarcar answered.

"There is another question who bear me in doubt. Why the humans are cast so far to this system with inhabitable planets nearby but many of the species which the guardians created in their own solar system are only two years maximum apart from their living planets if using our human spaceship to travel." Maxter requested.

"There is a tragic event which led to your race being stranded here. You will know eventually." Pazarcar replied and they both headed to the square for the ceremony.

Chapter 5

In the square there are military choirs band perform the tunes and the people were gathering around. The Police and Military personnel are setting up watch post for conducting searches for people carrying camera and high tone items. In addition there are two helicopters patrolling around the sky. Many reporters and camera men arrived to witness the event and live streaming to their employed stations.

"Why the humans would love such an noisy atmosphere with. It is so unbearable for us. Should we activate the shield?" Calok asked.

"No, we will see how they reduce such noise later. The humans loves merry at such a crucial circumstances." Pazarcar commented.

Meanwhile the choir has been brought to silence. The event host, Mr Malcolm went to the stage for an announcement.

"Today we celebrate a new era for mankind who will reached their full potential in a near future. Today we will honor the visitors who spared no bigger effort for the humans to thrive upon themselves. They come in peace and ready to give humans a new demographic in all aspects. I shall pass my speech to the Galaxy Ambassador who will convey the messages to this world. Let welcome Mr Maxter, the galaxy ambassador." Mr Malcolm announced.

Maxter went up the stage and hold the microphone.

"It was a honor for me to advocate treaty for this planet. This world is rumbling with excitement and frenzies around every corner during the last few days. I am glad that I could handle this humans and star visitors affairs appropriately despite that I am a newbie in external relation matters." Maxter announced.

Meanwhile some protesters went out in front of him and a woman approaches him.

"Your poor abilities and curiosity will be leading my son to his death. It is all because of your obedience towards them which we have to fight a heavy war that led many families without a heir." A woman shouted out.

"We have the Heir Protection Policy and it should be sufficient to protect all our descendants. I am a bachelor and is willing to put my family line in peril with many soldiers regardless of marital status. I have set an example."Maxter announced.

"Not everyone as selfless as you. If one of your woman born you a retarded child to you then will be still proud of your family line and do you think children without fathers are pleased with their family life." Another war protestor shouted.

"Now calm down everyone. There is a great future for earth and if we squabble around, then humanity will be slow to adapt to future circumstances for a much greater galaxy. Humans will languishing behind other races having to restrict to earth itself and its inhabitable planets around the solar system. Earthlings will be despair at such calamities and violent crimes which might arise. We will be paying a heavy price if humanity are to pit against other species in the future." Maxter suggested.

"We already have lost relatives to our own war and we wanted peace eternally. Now you wanted us to fight an unpredictable war. A newbie ambassador like you has done a great misdeed for the people of Earth. Stop playing like a messenger to us for those deities." Another protester shouted.

"You all have misinterpreted my missions in this deal, I have try to compromise the pact more favorable to us the humans." Maxter announced.

"We have enough of his intolerable nonsense. Now lets tear his stage apart." A protester urging the others.

The crowd moved forwards and the security could not stem them who block them with the shields. Eventually one of the crowd push forward and tripped the wire, many fall and the stage holding the microphone fell and a high frequency tone is heard. Pazarcar, Calok and Lacus find its tone unbearable and shouted out their voice which causes electromagnetic frequency interruption. The helicopters on the sky twist their movement and the pilots found it is uncontrollable.

"What is going here?" The reporter aboard the chopper asked.

"Tighten your seat belts we are going down if we do not retract this chopper to the ground." The pilot shouted.

"Why we need to do this?" The reporter asked.

"You will start praying if we have to put up with your persistence questioning." The co-pilot shouted after trying hard to manipulated.

The siren tone from the aliens drove the pilot and its choppers towards the area, the reporter's camera was swinging away from the reporter who grabbed it by the snap button which immediately snaps a photo on the star visitors with its flashlight. Pazarcar, Lacus and Calok left in a rage of anger and immediately enter their shuttle.

"What are they doing?" Lex asked.

"Get away you stupid visitors." A protester throw a disconnected microphone towards the saucer shield but deflected.

The saucer lifted itself up and fires a beam which melts the protestors.

"They are killing the protestors. Bravo One and two, commence firing till hostilities cease." The helicopter pilot chided another via code word.

The choppers fired their missiles but it deflected its shots towards the protestors causing more casualties. The saucer remains invincible with the shield remain intact.

"Oh my god, their shields remains impenetrable. What should we do?" The helicopter pilot asked.

"Concentrated the fire on one particular spot." The commander urged.

The saucer sends out search discs who will locate their target at will however it does not have shield protection although it is fast and able to elude projectiles firing. Meanwhile the body guards on the ground starts to arm their pistols and firing at the saucer and its discs while taking up a cover behind a building.

One of the discs reshape its outer metal and flew through a building and eventually killed some of the guards, then the guards tried to force themselves out of their cover. Johnny upon seeing the guards being killed draws out his pistols and began to start shooting at the discs.

Meanwhile the saucer began to disappear gradually and only left the discs to battle against the earth helicopters.

One of the disc damaged a helicopter and it is crashes down killing a few spectators. Next another disc flew towards the humans who fired from their cover position at high speed. Johnny run out of pistols bullets and begin to snatch a rifle from a fallen comrades around his vicinity.

"Those are artificial machines who have less intelligence than a living flesh beings." Johnny commented.

"If it is the truth, then we can distract him using duplicates." Hobby replied.

"What's your plan?." Johnny asked.

"A mirror, they recognized only human from faces or movement. They may not be able to calculate the thickness from the front and could determine that it is a fake." Hobby replied.

The two bodyguards then searched around a nearby wardrobe shop for a mirror. The rest of the bodyguards and police battle the two discs as ejected by the saucer.

Next another disc is flying upwards and fires a particle beam which destroyed the truck by firing its beam the fuel tank which kills a few more people. The disc trying to attack the other helicopter but it missed and the latter fired its machine but the former avoided the shots. Next the disc changes its shape and fire its beam like a cannon which terminates more people. The Helicopter pilot lock on the target with main armament missile and pushes the fire button, but the transformed discs could roll at steep angle which the missiles could not follow and it detonated against a building.

"They are beyond our missile orientation which is too steep." The helicopter pilot observed.

Meanwhile Johnny set up a mirror which could hold a discs attention so that they could fire at the target well. While trying to haul the mirror towards the battle zone to distract the discs, the crew faces the onslaught of the flying discs, the soldiers trying to avoid the beam of the discs collide with the mirror and it falls down causing the mirror to be shatter and the glass is splinter.

"Our ideas got burst, what should we do again?" Hobby shouted.

"We got to seek out another plan." Johnny replied.

Meanwhile one of the disc fired another beam which devastated the furniture around and everyone around there was hit unconscious.

Maxter was trapped between the protestors and the wooden plank, but he still trying to crept out of the debris. Johnny finds a radio link system which will communicate with the air units around. He finds three soldiers who was hiding behind the debris and shooting at the second disc.

"There is a construction area nearby and a dug trench we need to sneak out from here and run towards there. " Johnny suggested.

"We have no cover over there and our weapons have not effect on them." Sergeant Frank answered.

"We have a radio link system here. We can made dummy runs to distract its attention and our units would strike it down with heavy armaments." Johnny requested.

"It is a good idea. Now boys get to the trench immediately." The sergeant ordered.

The soldiers finally reached the trench and began to fire at a disc to attract its attention. Johnny called out a helicopter nearby to battle the units while the soldier ran inside the trench to attract the attention. While Johnny calling out air supports, a soldier was burned by the beam fired the disc.

"Air units on the sky, we require your assistance. We are diverting one of the flying discs attention and we need your heavy shot which will blast that shaped metal dirt out of the sky." Johnny requested.

"Roger that, we will proceed to your coordinates and destroy that." The helicopter pilot Mag answered.

Finally, the trick works for Johnny and Sergeant Frank. The disc have trouble switching targets around and was distracted by the multiple bullets flying around. But the disc have destroyed the trench and made it hard to run again. A Corporal collides with the sergeant and both are down. The disc find them and prepare to fire the beam which is gathering energy after discharging a beam. Finally the helicopter appears and fired its missiles towards the disc and it exploded.

"We finally crushed one of them." The helicopter pilot shouted in jubilant.

"Proceed to destroy the next disc. It is on the other side of that building." Johnny speaks to the pilot with the radio link system.

The soldiers obeyed and they come across the next street where the disc is giving the ground forces a hard time for them to aim at the target. Eventually Johnny and Sergeant

Frank try to outwit the disc by making dummy run across it and shooting it around. The disc decided to chase after Frank who hides from the wall. It arrived over a truck where there is a lamp post above it. Johnny's quick wit allowed him to fire a bullet in the fuel tank of the truck and its explosion blew the truck up to squash the disc. It temporarily damaged its engine system and one its legs. It then open up a hatch and brings up a tube for repairing its legs. Sergeant Frank fired his rifle and damages its repair system. Finally Johnny alerted the helicopter who fired its missiles completely destroying the disc again.

"We finally got rid of those hostile visitors." Pilot James elated.

Suddenly a string of beams from a visible direction appeared and destroy the helicopter which burst into flames from an invisible element which revealed later as the visitors saucer and they unleashed more powerful beams which burn out more ground troops with their weapons. Johnny managed to evade the beam but the swing beams burn out his palm. The foreign leaders were certain that the visitors is going to wipe out the humans on this planet and the prime minister orders all people to leave.

Maxter finally climbs out of the debris and shouted with both of his hands up.

"No, do not harm the humans." Maxter pleaded.

Pazarcar knows Maxter is pleading for humans and he is obliged to help him.

"Activate the time siphoning operation. The humans are indispensable at such crucial time." Pazarcar ordered.

Lacus and Calok activated the switches from their invisible panel and their generator absorbs the winds which produce a large energy flow around the environment. Cars, trucks and even barricades are thrown into the air.

"Our generator is ready to expel the energies throughout every edge of this planet." Calok informed Pazarcar.

"These lame humans will finally understand further act of insolence will result in their total extermination. Unleashed the time wave energies." Pazarcar ordered.

Soon the energy waves seems to brush the world apart and it disrupts the electrical signal all around the world. Then in a sudden memory flash, all the crowds in the assembly area experienced a sudden flash of headache. Then everyone were frowning when they saw destroyed equipments at the surrounding.

Sergeant Frank saw his subordinates holding a burn out rifles.

"What is going out? Why are you holding a heavily burnout rifle?" He asked.

"It baffles me, but Sergeant your rifle and pistol holder are producing those odor smell. There are perforated spots all over." Corporal David answered.

Sergeant Frank looks at his burnt out armament and frowns upon what has happened.

"Sarge, look the choppers are down and pretty much destroyed, but the pilots and reporters look fine. What exactly has happened?" Corporal David asked.

"I cannot recall what has happened. Now get everyone in our platoon and assembled here." Sergeant Frank replied.

The corporal obeyed his command and carried out his task. Corporal Frank gets to Johnny who is also frowned by holding his cremated pistols in his hand. Maxter felt that this have happened before as he could recall an incident at the waste land.

"What exactly has happened? We felt that we are being burn alive before." Johnny asked.

"The Prime Minister and everyone are all right, but those destroyed equipments puzzled us." Sergeant Frank commented.

Maxter immediately checked on the Prime Minister and the foreign diplomats. He is surprised that he found the helicopter pilots alive but the helicopters are totally destroyed. He then walked to an old man who is using an antique video tape recorder for filming and took it away.

He managed to get home and run the video tape where he saw the devastation images wrought upon the star visitors. Later he saw how the visitors have the ability to turn everything back to normal. Maxter then run to the stadium and asked the visitors.

Maxter suddenly recalled that he also saw those lights when he try to manipulate the lights on the barren land to shine on the stars. Out of panic, he returned to the stadium and finds Pazarcar. The star visitors are packing their robotic device using the manipulating screen. Finally Maxter approached them.

"I know those equipment are being destroyed hostile weapons and the humans who are killed have been resurrected by you.

Is that the time wave process that your guardians always injected on certain humans on those past fifty earth years. I saw those lights before when I try to emit light source to your stars before I fainted. So my experiment is a success which inadvertently drew you here." Maxter asked.

"Indeed you grew wise and realized that you are the reason that we come here." Pazarcar replies.

"Why you are hiding the truth from me when I wanted the answer of the person who called upon you." Maxter questioned.

"Humans have finally have realized their potential and willing to explore extensively for an answer. It is a ripe time that humans need to find a new demographic for themselves rather than living in their improvised star system when you finally called upon us.. Regarding the incident that has erupted between us and your human race, do cast it aside and we need your race to come with us to the star system without prompt." Pazarcar commented.

"Our truce has not yet fulfilled between each other, it is an agreement that the three wishes are delivered in earth form." Maxter requested.

"Your humans are in no position to get a deal from us. Remember, we gave you advice on improving on your flying objects. We bestow you the second wish just now when you beg us not to kill more humans. Thirdly we have resurrected the humans that we just killed. That is three wishes that you wanted." Pazarcar commented.

"But the electro-magnetic shields and the new fuel source material. We need them." Maxter replied.

"Your failure to exert control over your race cause the human to lose the deals. You will obtained one upon successful negotiation with the Zarkano on forming peace on that system. Now get your humans ready, no more pleading for any requests from us." Pazarcar angrily said.

"I am not given the authority to placate the crowd. You should understand my supervising boundary." Maxter lamented.

"Inter species conflict should be resolved by the representatives of individual races. You cannot displayed such juvenile responsibilities and ignorance when the humans enter our solar system. More races will face their peril end from the Zarkano if you failed to exemplify enthusiasm leadership coordination with your race." Pazarcar says.

"Then I should seek for your forgiveness for my race's offensive altitude towards your party. Let continue our treaty as we need to deliver the gift to the humans." Maxter pleaded.

"The truce between us would resume if you could eliminate violence and cultivate peace in our galaxy. No more pleadings." Pazarcar advised.

"I will advocated with our leaders to terminate our deal. We humans could achieved inter stellar space flight in the future without your help. I will not travel with our troops to the your star system." Maxter comments.

"Ambassador, your space flight could not be achieved without any assistance from our alliance. Consult your strongest human faction in this planet. I shall not give any further explanation and would not accede to your pleadings. Now my only advice that you should prepared more effort for the journey to repaid us." Pazarcar commented.

"You exaggerated. Our human have achieved it on our own. What you said is only fictional that we always hear. In order to combat with those Zarkano Tribes, we need the other two wishes to be completed so that we can overcome their superiority." Maxter requested.

"Your human faction has been using our alliance knowledge to compete among themselves and create intense rivalry. Therefore our existence have been kept in controversy notes. I felt apologetic but we will not reverse our decision, you humans need to earn a deal with us. And no humans can back out of this deal or witness the catastrophic reaction that you witnessed. Extinction or continual advancement is an option that you should decide for your races with great consideration." Pazarcar commented.

Maxter walked away and heads its destination towards the Prime minister office and urge to meet with the Prime Minister. Winston agreed to former requests.

"Sir, I have a confession to make. The phenomenon event that you saw today is a result of the humans testing on the patience of the visitors, this video will leave you in awe of the visitors prowess." Maxter asked.

The Prime Minister saw the video and he is also baffled with the scene which seems to recall his memory.

"So the visitors have the abilities to alter our brain memory cells. Well it supposed that the kidnapping of the humans as reported are prove to be true." The Prime Minister asked.

"Yes, it could be. Our electronic equipment which may have record the incident could be erased too. They could use the same method of erasing human memory, but the present regime of the Guardians of Formation may not have any knowledge of the kidnapping of the humans for experimentation." Maxter answered.

The Prime Minister have some confusion with Maxter's answer but the latter continued his speech.

"Sir, the visitors have renounced their deals with us. I really need your help to convince the diplomats and leaders from other country. They told me that because of this incident, only one gift would be delivered and we have not maximized the potential of the gift." Maxter said.

"I am sure that they will aid us if we run into conflict with the other races of that star system. Well I have a plan to convince the diplomats and other leaders in such predicament. We told them that the aggressive race in the other solar systems will be battling another group of inferior beings and we are needed in that star system for negotiation to prevent them from committing another genocide. A war is inevitable for earth human in such situation. As we announce in the forum with our diplomats, the humans will gained nothing once those Zarkano subdue the existing inferior race on their galaxy." Prime Minister commented.

"I felt hurt because I realized I am the one who brought them here which is definitely a grave mistake." Maxter answered.

"I would like to hear how you led them here." The Prime Minister requested.

"There was a night that I read a book on a legend which illustrated a man trying to call upon the gods by lighting up six lights in a continuous circle so that they can see them. Then I saw a television program which a woman turns a laser pointer on six directions which will light up upon each successful detection. So I have the idea of trying out on a waste land using my big energy spot light. Next a light beams falls on me which you saw on the video acts like a time wave, but they implanted some organisms on my body and later when they came, those organisms are drawn out." Maxter asked.

"It is amazing that you solved this ancient mystery with just a small spot light. We have historians or archaeologists who are still struggling with the riddle. Well you are a true genius." The Prime Minister commented.

"Fiddle with the myth land me in such dilemma as I am leading many young man to their grave, especially my own countrymen who will cursed at me." Maxter lamented.

"Although some people will die but in the end many humans are saved. They will be grateful to you. The war is not in your forecast plan, you need to exonerate yourself for the huge casualties that you created in the future. Our country have the Heir Protection Policy which ensured every male has a heir before fighting in the war. Again if we humans were to fight another race, it could end the violence conflict between our human nations. In addition, peace among human will be more cohesive and you deeds have shined well with your curiosity. " Prime Minister praises Maxter.

"The visitors have come and I cannot alter the pact. The important concern for me is to seek minimal casualties for the humans in such large scale war so I can redeemed myself. I think the humans would end the war here but would possibility start a new battle on that star system." Maxter replied.

"War is inevitable as long there are greed and rivalry in living among our hearts. We could minimize the clashes between humans as much as possible through negotiation and diplomatic relation. Please do not reproached yourself." The Prime Minister requested.

"All right. I will definitely do my best for humanity." Maxter answered as he leave.

The next day, Maxter finally convinced all the foreign diplomats that the expedition team will be needed to stem the Zarkano aggression. He also assured that a negotiation will be held to pacify the Zarkano for a peace treaty.

During afternoon, Maxter pays a visit to the star visitors again. Pazarcar showed him a star map.

"Now if we were to go through the portal, there are several precaution you need to undertake. The portal will be activated for only fifteen earth minutes. You will need to double up your effort and plan your journey with the greatest wisdom. We calculated that your faster plane will passed through the journey successfully. But your bigger craft will not have a easy time. Look through your past or any inspiration that would help you overcome such hurdles." Pazarcar commented.

"Why only earth fifteen minutes but not longer?" Maxter asked.

"Because in the past, our alliance had irregular practice when teleport towards your planet. During their visit to this planet, there are unexpected materials which are brought back. We will remedy their mistakes. There are also rocks that will clash against you. They weigh a few hundred earth tons that your lightly armored planes could not sustain those damages." Pazarcar commented.

"What happens to the planes could not pass through the tunnel." Maxter asked.

"The sky and ground would meet each other together with no distinct distance." Pazarcar replied.

"It means gravity force would be at maximum and everything will be crushed." Maxter answered.

"That is correct." Pazarcar replied.

"I will need you to lend your effort for this." Maxter requested.

"We are not aiding you, it is left to your human ideas to work out during the journey. Your human have films which can instill your inspirations. However I shall give an advice, there is a lot of the breathing air inside which your humans needed. Do make use of such advantages." Pazarcar answered.

"We will try to overcome such obstacles. Where is the place of embarking?" Maxter asked.

Pazarcar emits an earth map screen through a metal worm object on the air and points to a location near Australia.

Maxter acknowledges the location and informed the visitors that they will be ready for the next two days. Pazarcar welcomed the decisions.

The next day, Maxter meets with Commander Tagrin at the air force base. Maxter showed the video of the portal tunnel which he filmed with Lex during yesterday conversation with Pazarcar. Maxter requested additional turbo jet engine to be fixed on the C-130 transport plane wings.

"Sir, it cannot be done. The fuselage could not have to be linked properly and no solid fixed design is available. Could you plead with them to extend the tunnel passage time?" Commander Tagrin requested.

"We are not given such lucrative duration. We cannot bring our heavy equipment along in case of a conflict if the extra rockets charger are not fixed. We could place missiles on top of it and drive them over for a test." Maxter suggested.

"That was not a good idea but it is still considered an attainable idea. All right guys please move that unwanted rockets and fixed those on the C-130 transport plane." Commander Tagrin ordered.

Finally a prototype is tested which succesfully passed its tests. Commander Tagrin was pleased.

"Then we will need more of this. We need more workers to work around the clock for all these transport planes to pin those turbo jet engine chargers on the wing." Maxter ordered.

Commander Tagrin dispel orders to the workers accordingly and wanted a inspection by tomorrow noon.

Meanwhile at the orbit of the planet Hisguro. Lorka and his star fleets have tracked the guardians movement through hidden tracking device on asteroids. At the commander flagship, a Karploit moved to the bridge with two twelve inch device wipe one attached at each corner. When it finally arrived, the Karploit raises its device wipe and brings out energy wave which forms a screen which shows some recordings. The vice commander Aloqi explained the findings on the screen.

"Commander, our hidden tracking device have been scouring the area for the past four days. They reported a mass movement of guardians activities from the vicinity of planet

Altro. Different shapes of saucer crafts are detected which means all races of the guardians could be assembled on that planet. However we have no knowledge of their motives on that planet." Aloqi explained.

"Why would they have such strange assembly on that remote planet? However that remote planet is a wonder area for testing our weapons. On my orders, set all ships to the destination to that planet immediately. All ship are to proceed in a slow manner. Use a ZealSeal to transport our spotters to planet to spy on them before letting our fleet penetrate the planet surface." Lorka ordered.

Aloqi sends out signal to all space ships which changes the fleet destination towards planet Altro.

Two days later, the sun is set. The expedition force led by Maxter and Commander Tagrin finally arrived by the shores of Australia. Maxter is seated in the C-130 transporter. Pazarcar and its crew finally activated the portal. The sky clouds finally groups together and morph into a blue hole with the clouds turning.

"It is nothing short of fantastic. They are able to create substance from air compound." Lex commented.

"Now is the time for jumping to new platform, jets take off and head towards that cloud." Maxter ordered.

Soon the jets scrambled towards the cloud and followed by the C-130 transporter. Pazarcar's ship holds the cloud with its energy wave. The fast combat jets enter the cloud. Finally all of the heavy transporters finally enter the portal and the cloud released its energy wave which forms back the white cloud.

"Now where are they?" The Prime Minister asked.

Chapter 6

The planes experienced a series of awkward flight in the portal.

"Turn the plane down and avoid those asteroids. Do not lose sight of the visitor's craft." Maxter ordered.

The pilot obeys his command and pulled the plane down.

Now the stones are getting in our way. The fast crafts have to be evacuated first." The commander argued.

"There was a light from the front." Lex pointed to the sky.

"Gather all fast traveling jets to made full speed towards the light. Not much time to waste. We have to ignite the turbo trusts." Maxter requested the Commander Tagrin.

"All jets are to activate their turbo thrust immediately and head towards the light which is place of destination." Commander Tagrin ordered.

The jets pilots obeyed and activated their turbo thrust towards the destination which leaves the heavy transporters behind.

"Now they are gone, we must activate our turbo charger to the maximum." Maxter ordered.

Commander Tagrin ordered all the heavy transports to activate the turbo thrusts and all it is flying fast towards the target, but Maxter transport plane hit a asteroids and the plane wings is damage along with its turbo thrusts.

"Sir what do we do, the plane is running with one less turbo thrusts." The pilot asked the commander.

"We need a force that can blow the air heavier so that we can have a higher thrust of force." Maxter commented.

"The asteroids combustion could help us if they could be blown off from the below." Commander Tagrin questioned.

"Even that will not be enough, our targeting direction is disoriented" Maxter answered and paused for a moment to observe the situation.

"Due to imbalance engine bursting and our plane is turning circles. I have a plan. Turn off all the supported turbo thrust. We will overload them to give them a higher starting engine push after the asteroids detonation." Maxter suggested.

"All right, pilot commander released a guided missile from below and target the back asteroids from the below. Co-pilot hold on the clutch engine thrust and allowed much oil for initial power up. When the asteroids are blew up, released them and stepped heavily on the fuels accelerator." Commander Tagrin ordered.

The pilot reversed the direction of missile launcher tube and fired it and the missile hit the asteroid causing the explosion and it gave a force and the co-pilot releases the clutch and pushes it accelerator. The plane accelerated at a high velocity and soon it reaches the portal on the other side. The portal closes and the crew felt relieved upon reaching the planet.

"We finally made it. This is a beautiful planet where its lush green surrounding are untouched by extensive artificial harassment." Commander Tagrin commented.

"Yes it is, but it will be dreadful if our planes do often travel to and from Earth. I will try to consult the visitors if we can extend the duration further upon completion of this negotiation." Maxter suggested.

Meanwhile Pazarcar's space craft have risen above Maxter transporter and telepathically called Maxter and informed him that he needs to follow them as the former had found them a landing zone.

"The visitors have found us a landing zone. Let's follow them." Maxter ordered.

Soon all of the planes followed the Pazarcar's craft which led them to encounter a large fleet of guardians saucers who just landed.

"Make our landing space on that large waste land besides the visitors fleet." Maxter ordered.

All the planes make their landing at the waste land. Pazarcar receives Maxter and his expedition team. Pazarcar used his finger and points to the location that they are residing using their hologram which display the planet. Maxter issues commands to refuel all planes and calibrate the navigating system according to the current position after obtaining the time duration from Pazarcar.

Once all the navigation systems on all planes have been calibrated. Commander Tagrin conducted the bomb dropping test and arranges for a dud bomb to be dropped from the planes to test its latitudes and longitudes coordinates. Everyone was pleased when the dud bomb lands precisely. Commander Tagrin praised the human's geographic reference basis could be apply on this planet as well but required a better precision decimal points of distance between each interval angle because of a larger planetary surface. Maxter proposed to send radio waves back to earth however Commander Tagrin disagreed with him.

"Sir, this planet is thirty nine light years from earth. It would take earth three million years to receive the messages. It might not reached earth because the signal might be lost over the milky way which might jammed the transmissions." Commander Tagrin argued.

"We have to inform earth even it they will receive the messages which is three million years late as we do not know what type of circumstances we are facing. Let the descendants of these men know that their grand daddy did land on an alien planet." Maxter answered.

"Your explanation sound correct. The signal will not send well from the ground area. We have to find a higher ground to send it." Commander Tagrin suggested.

"Well that hill looks likes a suitable position, gather some men and we will send the signal from that location." Maxter commented.

Commander Tagrin assembled about ten men and set out in two rovers. Among them comprised of Johnny and Lex who have squabbled with each other earlier on. On their way towards the mountain on two rovers. Johnny notices a sparkling red light and inform Maxter who immediately order all crew to be grounded and search for the light.

"There is a red light which contains sparkling qualities. I am sure it does not look like flesh beings which lie in a cower position."Johnny commented.

"It must be some of the advanced species that could have be manipulated those machines to monitor us. Our visitors are already here and they do not need such equipment to check our movement. Commander dispatched your men to search for it." Maxter ordered.

Johnny who is holding a rifle slowly proceeds towards the forest region with a hand held frequency detector device. He then turned the knob to a lower frequency and he soon walked towards the hidden robotic scout unit to trace the signal. The robotic scout unit found itself at a disadvantage and crawling backwards and submerge to the river nearby

"We are closing in. He is just ten meters away. Sir" Johnny commented.

Johnny and Lex overhears some river sound and advances further again. The red spotter moves back again and it steps on a large serpent reptile and accidentally wake up the latter with its eye open. Johnny and Lex are getting close towards the river however the handheld frequency detector could not detect the signal anymore. Lex unintentionally steps on a slippery object which is a small amphibian reptile with six legs and an enclosed duck bill mouth and with a horn in its mouth. The amphibians reptile was covered with giant leaf and it is two feet long. Lex was scared out of his wits and the reptile groaned and chased him. Lex jumps over it and slips. He falls into the river but he hold to a root of a tree.

Suddenly the large serpent who have a five meters by two meters wide jaw sprung out of the river with a raucous roar and a burst of the purple flame which erupt from the creature mouth. Johnny fires at the creature from the sides. The creature then submerged again which johnny could not see and raises itself to the land and knocking him down sideways with Johnny gun in the creature mouth. The creature have a double row of teeth on the upper and lower side of the mouth and crush the gun into pieces. Next the creatures climbs and inch himself closer towards Johnny. Johnny tries to roll but the creature forward its jaw and grab his water bottle which in turn pulls Johnny. Maxter and an American soldiers arrives and fired at the creature head and body from twenty meters but to no avail. Just as creature is ready to pull Johnny to the river, Lex fired his rifle to the creature legs and inflicting hurt to its leg and the creatures quickly released Johnny but the creatures fall crumbles the root branch which Lex held on. The latter moves his hand and tried to grabs the river edge. The gun sound and the creatures led other smaller size creatures which belong to the same species of the previous predator to swim towards towards Lex. Maxter and the American fires at the rivers which Lex could not grab the edge and he switch his hands towards another tiny root back with one hand. Johnny immediately raced to Lex aid and grab his hand. The predators were swimming fast and one was near Lex and opened its jaw which is beaten back by Maxter's rifle but more are coming as Maxter could not aimed at them fast enough. Johnny managed to raise Lex up slowly but a predator is gaining first on him and open his jaws but Captain Nigel, an American soldiers toss a grenade into the creature mouth. Lex's leg submerge itself back and a detonation is heard. The creature's body is dismembered and the surrounding predators swallows its remains.

"Thanks for your helping hand." Lex said.

"If not for you, I will have become shredded meat for that huge predator." Johnny suggested.

"That was lucky, we are even now." Lex suggested.

"This is a sweet way to end your squabbling for two of you. Any sign of that red emitting machine." Maxter announced.

"It was at the bottom of the lake after being spit by the creature. We need underwater equipment to carry out a search on this muddy water." Johnny answered.

"It looks like a huge eight legged spider which possess metallic surface qualities. It freaks me out if we have to see that large predator again." Lex suggested.

"It is too dangerous to seek that machine out. The surrounding is full of giant trees and leafs. It resembled prehistoric earth where trees are tall and animals are enormous like dinosaurs. We have no knowledge how many of us will perish before one of them are fallen. It is no way that we will sacrifice any precious lives to look for that mobile robotic object." Maxter commented.

"In addition, victims of that predator suffered an extreme horrific death with those sharp multiple teeth piercing through the bones." Lex added.

"Now let proceed on to that hill to send the transmission back to earth." Maxter suggested.

The second rover team finally arrived at the hill where it is meet by the Commander Tagrin rover.

"Sir, we encountered a large ape about six meters tall on a greater height. It will be very unwise to approach them as they are unpredictable. Should we sent our boys to flush them out with our guns." Commander Tagrin commented.

"No, the guardians will not appreciate our policy for killing non deadly inferior beings. We should show favor to them so that they will not harm us. Any people here who have cultivate good relation with earth monkeys." Maxter answered.

An African American soldier Jim Brown stands out from the crowd and speaks to Commander Tagrin.

"I have a pet chimpanzee and he likes banana. Sadly we did not bring them here but they like chips." Jim Brown answered.

"We have some packets here and that will do the trick. Now let meet them. Have the guns point down. Let hope they are omnivorous. " Maxter suggested.

Meanwhile the team reached the level where they meet the giant apes which have hairy and all over the bodies. They looked like orangutan but have the muscular body structure of a gorilla. Their legs could stand upright and they have rounded muscles at their arm pit. When they saw the humans they walk forward to meet them. Maxter called them out and he pull out his hand to shake the ape.

"We came in peace and we will not hurt you." Maxter said as he raised his hand and speaks with a microphone.

The creature was curious about the humans and he noticed the humans have five fingers which is the same as them. He then stretch his hand forward in order to shake Maxter hand.

"This is correct, we mean no harm. I need a packet of chips from some of you." Maxter ordered.

A Chinese soldier passed him a packet and Maxter put the chips into the ape hand and requests the ape to enjoy.

The ape tasted it and found the goodies satisfactory. Maxter commanded the rovers to give the ape the entire potato chips packages. Commander Tagrin then set up the communication devices and prepare to send the radio wave across.

"We are now at the planet Altro thirty nine light years from earth. We descended to this place at fifteen of May on the year 2015. Anybody who receive this message will need to tell earth that we are the first human to travel who set foot on another alien planet." Commander Tagrin transmitted the message to earth.

Meanwhile on the planet atmosphere of Altro, Vice Commander reported their findings to Commander Lorka at the starship.

"Commander, our probes have found the area where the guardians have landed. We have discover flying objects which we cannot identified. They are not in our list of familiar guardian saucers. In addition, we find some new intelligence life which we never encountered before. I suspect those unknown flying objects belong to these new species." Vice Commander Aloqi commented.

"Quick show me how they looks like. " Lorka ordered.

The probes then connected its probes to the screen input and Lorka inspect with amazement.

"It must be the guardians new species which they hide from us all along. Their machines seems free of energy beams material. We need to acquire more information on them." Lorka explained.

"When we defeat the guardians using the web, these new species will beg for our mercy. One of our scouts have also discovered such species strange vehicle and sent its information to us before its demise. It has four round objects which enabled it to move." Aloqi commented as he shows the image of Maxter land rover.

After watching the images on the screen. Lorka boasted that the new species will never match their capabilities, however he cautioned Aloqi that the new species must not be underestimated.

By noon, the bases and the planes are refueled. Members of the Guardians Formation have already established a communication with the Zarkano. Pazarcar and Calok went to the human base and search for Maxter, Vice Commander Rinco approached them to acquired what the former wanted and Pazarcar shows the hologram of Maxter. Commander Rinco next tries to contact Commander Tagrin that the star visitors requires his presence.

"I have acknowledged the command. Kindly send a chopper to fetch the ambassador as we tried to transmit information towards earth." Commander Tagrin ordered.

Meanwhile a helicopter had arrived and Maxter climbs aboard. A helicopter pilot saw the ape and questioned a radio operator.

"Are those ape harmful." The helicopter pilot asked.

"No, they are affable and omnivorous. Do not antagonize them." The radio operator urged.

The ape looks at the helicopter with surprise especially with the blades swinging and used his finger to turn a large circle. The other ape also shake his head later. Johnny found the apes are amusing.

"What are they doing?" Johnny asked.

"Maybe you can asked Jim, he know apes more than anybody else." Commander Tagrin answered.

Maxter arrived at the base and the visitors welcomed him to the star visitors shelter which is formed by electromagnetic shield. Maxter meets the other guardians races which are the Cerotine and the Drometalian.

The Drometalian Leader who have reptilian eyes goes forward and speak to Maxter.

"I am Axerian. Finally the humans are back in this star system after spending many millenniums in the other solar system. It is time for the humans to make contribution to this galaxy." The Drometalian leader Axerian speaks.

"We understand, helping the habitats on this star system which also benefit the people of Earth." Maxter answered.

"Now we have arranged a meeting with a top Zarkano leader. You still have much to learn. Earth ambassador." Pazarcar asked.

"Advocating peace with the Zarkano will greatly quell the violence on this star system. We have no opinions in which the Zarkano fight among themselves but they stand united and found the other inferior species an obstacle to their conquest. Hurting other species lives violates the creators agenda." Axerian commented.

"We must persuade them to enter a negotiation to keep this galaxy peaceful." Maxter asked.

"It will be great that they could co-exists with every species in peace. It will not stains our hand to fight them. Now human, the Zarkano external diplomat chief Desories is online. Have a seat at the gravity power chair." Axerian commented.

Maxter slowly taken a seat at the gravity power chair.

"Would there be a hindrance in language translation. They cannot understand our language and I cannot understand theirs." Maxter asked.

"No worry lad, every words from him will be translated to your known language via the our Leimuga. It is a translation device which will focus on your face with its deforming electrode imaging substance when you speak. It will be perfect English for your ears. Your English will also be translated to their language perfectly." Axerian commented.

"Diplomat Desories, we seek an audience with you on one of our spacecraft which was recently lost on your planet vicinity." Pazarcar requested.

"Who were the guardians that gone missing?" Desories asked.

"Senator Ankoro, his vice commander Polexi and the newly trained pilot Nicsers. They have previously deterred your race ambition for the planet of Roxan, the Serfornies homelands. Now submit them to us." Pazarcar speaks.

"We have no knowledge of your missing spacecraft. Our weapons lack capabilities to overpower your shields and does damage to any of your craft, however we will still extend our greatest cooperation with you to search for the missing saucer." Desories explained.

"Stop feigning your ignorance in front of us. We will investigate again and will not rest till their scalps are found." Pazarcar angrily requested.

"Senator Pazarcar, I am afraid to incur your displeasure. The trainee pilot Nicsers might have plunge the spaceship into any portal or oblivion in the state of panic. Our numerous forces could help you to search for them if the secret of the portal is reveal to us." Desories commented.

"The portal is your ulterior interest. We will find this universe at risk if we accept your aid. Now the guardians demanded that you withdrew expedition that proves to be detrimental towards other inferior species." Axerian requested.

"The Ogerila tribes breath dangerous toxic when they speak and their surroundings are full of predators which hurt us. We need their resources and Ogerilla species has many difficulties for its usage because of their limbs location which plagued their movement. So we spared them the misery and burn them out. This could give better usage to other species in the galaxy. Perhaps the guardians could give them a capable biological structure and spare them from performing tormenting movement." Desories answered.

"We do admit that the guardians should overhaul the Ogerilla biological structure formation. The Zarkano should not have send them to extinction. However the Serfornites were deprived of those handicapped movement, but why are they receiving horrendous action from your forces. They have done your species no wrong." Axerian asked.

"Those savages clowns trying to fool us during our pact. We change and made the deal to suit our needs. They are lazy and arrogant, but those imbecile fools wanted a bigger pie in our truce which enraged our good will." Desories answered.

"Perhaps more diplomatic relations time are needed and this will help to heal the indifference between both parties and result in less conflict which could claimed lives." Maxter explained.

Desories have his screen switched and he looked at Maxter with surprise. He sent a transmission towards Lorka Starship which receives a transmission and the Karploit put the signal to Commander Lorka screen.

"I have not seen your races before. What are you and where do you come from?" Desories asked.

"I am a human and my name is Maxter. I am here on a diplomatic mission from the planet Earth to seek an eternal peace with your race in this galaxy." Maxter announced.

Lorka is surprised and conclude the strange machinery could belong to the humans.

"We humans have seen war between ourselves in the past and it causes catastrophic lives which only brings sadness. Only by frequent diplomatic communication and adequate self defence could bring peace for both parties." Maxter announced.

"How do you bargain with us? Do your race creates worm holes or have large star cruiser?" Desories asked.

"Our space age is primitive compared to yours. And we have not landed our people on another planet. But we could still trade on our substance like food, medical knowledge. Conquest is not a solution that you should seek permanently." Maxter answered.

"I noticed your race are more advanced than those species that we previously encountered. However I do not see your race as equal to us. Your race still needs more practical innovation to obtain a single deal from us." Desories asked.

"Our machines may not be not your equal but it will still give yours a laborious effort to tame us. We will try to protect the inferior species here. Such conflict will not give you much gain, Your Excellency. It is unwise to incur the precious lives of your species for such war." Maxter requested.

"Arrogant human, we will not changed our agenda and will await your challenge much ahead. Let's hope you will give us a tough time or we will dozed off with a quick and easy victory over your race." Desories answered.

Lorka and Aloqi both laughed with humor.

"These arrogant human will receive reprisal for testing our patience." Aloqi commented.

"Desories your Excellency, I hope you will reconsider our offer carefully. There could be lot of benefits for both of us. With the guardians aiding us, the human race will not be a pushover and the war will dragged on causing heavy casualties on both sides." Maxter answered.

"Spare it human. We do not deal with such lowly beings like you." Desories said as he ends the transmission.

"It seems like a war is inevitable. They seem confident and quickly dismiss us as weak. Now we need to know when they will strike. How powerful are their shields as compare to yours." Maxter asked.

"Zarkano Shield technology is developed at a primitive stage. Like our shield, their shield and their power source are inseparable. Once their craft has low power, the shields are down. Strike on their fuel system. The shield will be disabled as they need to reignite the power fuel system. If your arsenal proved could strike them at high velocity on their fuel system could blow their craft apart. Another method will be splashing large heavy heat on the craft, the heavy heat will disrupt the shields causing dispersing, subsequent large explosion will again blow the craft apart. Thirdly striking them with a heavy object in multiple of their weight will also weight down the shields and crush their craft. Their smaller craft has less powerful shield as compare to their larger starship and possess soft metal for protection. In addition, it requires an irreplaceable energy fuel system however their energy usage is much efficient than yours. Their fuel system also provides their arm system. They also have energy supplied robotic machinery which could channel fuel remotely. There will be more energy loss if the target is at longer distance." Axerian explained.

"The Zarkano seems ready to ignore our yearns for peace. But they are not foolish to strike at us as they knows our abilities and strength." Pazarcar commented as Axerian speaks to Maxter again.

"Lad, the Zarkano have been relatively untested against a species with advanced machines. Give them a tough fight and it could lead them to sow peace in this Galaxy." Axerian commented.

"I hope they will change their mind for a diplomatic pact if I could conduct another round of conference with Zarkano's external diplomat Desories. More effort is required to tame their conquest ambition." Maxter explained.

"Nice effort lad, work harder to achieve a peace pact and this universe will be much safer." Axerian answered.

Meanwhile a sand storm has approached. Commander Brag tests the wind speed using a device and verified that the storm velocity is very fast.

"Sir the sandstorm is approaching and it surpassed the most fastest tornado on earth." Maxter asked.

"Cover up the planes and command all personnel are to stay refuge in the transporter. Send a transmission to Commander Tagrin to stay in the mountain till the sand storm is over." Maxter ordered.

Once Maxter gets inside the transport plane, he immediately conducted a briefing for the crews.

"Once the sandstorm is over, we have to be on Battle Station. The Zarkano leader rejects our first peace pact. I have to alter another treaty for those rogue species. In an event the pact failed to reach an agreement again. It could mean war and we will be expending large human casualties that even surpassed the human most cruel conflict." Maxter announced.

Meanwhile at the command ship of the Zarkano Fleet. Lorka turns to Aloqi.

"Exterminating the Guardians is an important task. The humans are are not our grave concerns unless they displayed serious retaliation. Prepare the ezyeme web for charging. Descend our starships into the guardians area. Once the sandstorm ended, we will become the masters of this galaxy." Lorka laughed.

In the midst of the sandstorm, Maxter went outside to look for Pazarcar.

"Pazarcar, I wanted to know what Zarkano wants. Could I know their likes and dislikes so that we can make better deals with them." Maxter asked.

"You could have the permission granted as used on the knowledge console. Ambassador, your effort will be futile and war is inevitable. A less sophisticated race will seldom be impressed and coerced by a highly advanced civilization to accede to the former demands. We will still guide your race to victory on this galaxy." Pazarcar commented.

"The people of earth will always be your greatest ally. I have a favor, I need a full understanding of the Zarkano but this console could only grant me a little amount of the knowledge of the Zarkano in one earth day. Our time is limited, I learn to learn more in a shorter period." Maxter answered.

"An injection of the costrolips is possible to learn from the Zakarno faster, however it do pose a trouble for your human bodies as it needs an exchange of your vital nerve axon of neurons which the costrolips will duplicate. However you must relieve the costrolips within a period of fifteen earth hours back to our console system or it will slowly cripple your brain nerves and articulate systems as your human biological system are not suitable for using this air liquid systems. You could command a saucer or speak to us even we are in the sleep even at long distance. You are the first human who are experimenting with the costrolips." Pazarcar speaks.

"How do I relieved the costrolips?" Maxter asked.

"Just think like removing the costrolips and the our console could simply remove it with its tube. The main substance of the costrolips could be used to channel strength to others in critical situation and the tube would only pick up if the this substance is present in your body. This in turn leads the secondary substance out of the veins." Pazarcar answered.

"Does it contains any side effects to the body if the main substance is missing?" Maxter asked.

"On the guardians body. It will decrease life span. But on your human body, it will cohabit with good cells and turn them into toxic blobs which will sever your veins. Death will followed." Pazarcar answered.

Meanwhile the Zarkano fleet uses their cloak flying robots to create invisibility for their starship before entering the planet surface.

When the Zarkano arrives three thousand miles from the landing base. They found numerous flocks of large alien birds called the hassenflaug accidentally bumps on their starships because of cloaking. Three of them enter the fuselage of the star fleet and causes disruption which stops all the light temporarily.

"Sir, a few of those flying creatures slip through and are attacking our fuel premises but we driven them off and a single engine needs repair." Aloqi reported.

"Our forces cannot take this any longer. Uncloak the vessels and turn those nasty flying creatures into ashes. Use the concentrated ray." Lorka ordered.

"But our energy will be depleted if we used those rays. Recalled the pilots." Aloqi asked.

"No, it is too risky to lose the pilots and there are too many of those creatures." Lorka answered.

The Zarkano fleet fired their concentrated rays from the round turret and whip it across the sky which kills a lot of flying hassenflaug. This spurs the other flying creatures to fly away from the zone. The Zarkano fleet energy ran low after the flying creatures dispersed. Lorka ordered the fleet to be cloaked again and ran full speed ahead.

Chapter 7

Meanwhile at the console, Maxter found no deficiencies in Zarkano political structures but concluded to be dictatorship over its people. He also found Zarkano vehicle to be highly maneuverable but found that they could have weak armor if the shields are lost which fits with Senator Axerian description.

Senator Ankoro wakes up with little lethargy and immediately activated the distress signal which will transmit to the alliances. Unable to move up, he fell unconscious again.

Calok, Axerian and Senator Trulog found themselves in dilemma after their celestial device found traces of approaching heat emitting from sky on the planet. However the cloaking Zarkano could not be detected on their image scanners. However the incoming distress signal from Senator Ankoro shares the same location as the position as pointed out by the image scanners.

"Ankoro's distress emitting signal came from the those invisible objects. But they are nowhere to be found." Senator Trulog asked.

"Use the anti cloaking system to examine the suspecting area." Axerian suggested.

The anti cloaking system was able to detect the outer schematic of the cloaking objects which reveals an outline Zarkano capital ship with its scanners movement of its air motion.

"The Zarkano had arrived on this planet. They thought they can evade themselves by cloaking. Now they are trying to deliver Senator Ankoro's ship back to us where they hide it at their capital ship." Trulog suggested.

"Those crafty Zarkano must be trying to ambush us, they will be caught them off guard this time when we approached them. Inform Pazarcar and we followed his advice." Axerian advised.

Calok uses the console and a hologram appears at Maxter console which shows Calok. Pazarcar detected Calok's requests and went to the consoles in a hurry.

"We have discovered the Zarkano nearby along with Senator Ankoro." Calok suggested.

"Fetch the saucer and we will meet them." Pazarcar ordered.

Maxter also informed the Commander Rinco without haste about the incoming of the Zarkano Fleet. Commander Rinco called upon all the personnel to be ready for battle station.

When Calok's spaceship arrived over the human bases, Pazarcar is raised by the spaceship through its emitting light source and the men watched with amazement.

"Wish our chopper raise us like them?" An American soldier speaks.

Soon the guardians' saucers activated their shields and meet up with the Lorka Zarkano fleet. A lead ship by Senator Trulog stands out and move its ship towards Lorka starship.

"Show yourself, Zakano. Unless you wanted to face the full fury of the guardians. Halt your ships movement promptly. Hand over Senator Ankoro's ship on the capital ship behind you." Senator Trulog urged.

"Commander, They have locate us, but the eyzeme web have been fully charged." Aloqi commented.

"Have the eyzeme scorners surrounded them. They will be complacent with their shields. We will amuse them by uncloaking ourselves." Lorka ordered.

The Zarkano Forces finally switch off their cloaking systems which reveals Lorka and their ships towards the guardians.

Aloqi finally ordered his men to stop supplying the energy for the cloaking device and the fleet is finally visible to the Guardians ships.

"Senator Trulog, we are powerless to hide Senator Ankoro ship in our fleet. You are making a great mistakes." Lorka answered towards Senator Trulog.

"Commander Lorka, their distress signal came from your Capital Ship. Our guardians non radioactive communication transmissions could not be duplicated by the Zarkano. As usual you are trying to extract more secrets from their damaged ship. Now power down your ship and surrendered your forces immediately. We will take custody of your ships till your aggression nature is dissolved. You will face unexpected reprisal if you fail to be in compliant with our terms." Senator Trulog urged.

"Yes, Ankoro ship is in our custody. Power down yes but not mine but yours. Activate the eyzeme web." Lorka speaks as ordered Aloqi

Soon the eyzeme fired released its energy and the guardians saucer shield absorbs the electrostatic effects. The shields retract back to the energy source device and produce a reaction which knocks the unconscious crew. Soon all the guardians saucers descend to the ground.

However Pazarcar saucer arrived later and they are shocked when the guardians' saucer fell from the sky.

"What happened? All the ships are down. Let turn back to the human base." Lacus urged.

Pazarcar agreed with him and return the saucer to the human position.

"Aloqi, your bait was excellent. Senator Ankoro's ship distress signal saved us the burden of ambushing the Guardians." Lorka speaks as he praised Aloqi.

Aloqi spotted one saucer was getting away and give orders to cloaked itself and give chase.

Meanwhile Maxter and Vice Commander Rinco are studying the radar and found it weird that only a ship is returning and a group of objects are behind the fast dot. Maxter asked Vice Commander Rinco on advice of the battle outcome. The latter suggested an aerial reconnaissance would be necessary and Maxter agreed. Soon a search drone plane is launched to find out what have happened.

The search plane has detected a saucer but the group of flying objects could not be found. Pazarcar's saucer arrived at the human base fired an energy beam towards a sky area. The Zarkano fleet show its visibility and the humans ground weapons immediately fired. Pazarcar saucer was down when the eyzeme web spread its energy effects which the former absorbs the energy.

The Zarkano launched a large number of probes which face the humans. The Karploit have no shields against the humans, however they are not knocked off with just a bullet. A Bulgarian hit the optics eye of the probes and it erupt in a purple smoke. The anti aircraft guns blast a few probes but was eventually destroyed by a Zealseal pilot. Maxter managed to evade a Karploit chase and it led him to the tent. He managed to hit the Karploit a few times but did not come down as the Karploit body could deflect the bullets. He found his pistols ammunition has emptied and felt frustrated. Maxter tries to hid from a tree and found a spade left behind by his men. Maxter saw an ammunition pack on the table and throw the spade at the Karploit but the latter destroy it to half with the metal part still hit its optics rendering in a faint mode for a short while. Maxter race to the table and grab the ammunition pack. He hit the Karploit arsenal but the Karploit could still fire but the accuracy heads sideways and destroys a cable which exposes the live wire. The Karploit heads towards Maxter in a fast speed and its left arm pull out a drill like object. Maxter raised a table as a shield but the fast speed is too great for him to handle and Maxter is forced down. However the drill stuck in the table. Maxter immediately gets up and grab the live wire and put it into Karploit's eyes, heavily burning it and finally it was deactivated.

However expedition force surrendered quickly. A group of Zarkano soldiers marched to the tent and Maxter is surrounded and forced to surrender.

"Hands up Human and come with us." The Zarkano soldiers speaks up.

Lorka descended to the ground on a ZealSeal craft. He inspect the human equipments and aircraft and looked on with curiosity. Aloqi and his men brought out the language interpreter device along. This is used to decipher the conversation between the humans and the Zarkano.

When Maxter arrives with the guards, Lorka greet him.

"So you are the human leader in this sector. We saw you having a conversation with Desories our external diplomat. The Guardians Formation are defeated and you could really gave us a tough time if not for our sudden appearance. Maybe we would consider an alliance with us." Lorka asked.

"The Guardians gave us life and if you are really repentant, all these foolish war must be end immediately." Maxter requested.

"So your people are devoted slaves to them." Lorka answered as the Zarkano soldiers laughed.

"Evil will reap unexpected heavy retribution. Wars are not a solution to gain complete obedience, it will only lead to more suffering and create negative affection of your people. Your people will feel disgusted by your cruel action and this will leads to a strife civil war." Maxter requested.

"That only applies to your human species but our race are united. We will test some of your weapons. Your weapons appearance have really impressed me." Lorka speaks as he accepted a human made rifle from a Zarkano guard.

He then holds the rifle butt on his right hand and holding the rifle front on the left hand. He then pressed the trigger shots and hold on. The rifle fires continuously and the same concentrated fire destroys a Karploit by penetrating its metal.

"It is a loud and noisy weapon but its continuously fire impressed me. Our Karploit will take more than one hit to be down, however against flesh beings it will be very useful." Lorka suggested.

A Zarkano soldier later passed Lorka a shot gun. Lorka tested it by firing another shot at the Karploit and was threw a few meters away and was blew up with purple smoke arise.

"Your weapon is impressive but its arsenal have to be replaced rapidly thus made it less efficient as ours." Lorka asked.

"You should think thrice of waging a sustainable war before facing the full fury of the guardians and the rest of the species." Maxter warned but Lorka turned a deaf ear to him.

Meanwhile the Zarkano soldiers also captured Pazarcar, Lacus and Calok who were in their semi conscious state and creeping out from their saucer.

On the hill, Commander Tagrin attempt to make contact with the base having saw unidentified large alien craft over the base area and smoke is seen.

"Sir what happens now. Why are you not responding? I am Commander Tagrin." Commander Tagrin asked.

"Who are you and where are you now?" Lorka asked.

Meanwhile Pazarcar and his companions are marched towards the prison.

"Listen to me Earth. We need ammunition and men. Use the largest space craft to transport them to here so that we can fought a large scale war." Maxter speaks in a pretense tone.

"Now, what are you saying Sir." Tagrin asked.

Tagrin's group is baffled by Maxter's answer. Lex finally knows Maxter's intention and quickly stop Tagrin from answering.

"They are being held captive and so Maxter spoke in a different manner to deceive the enemy." Lex speaks softly.

"Sir our planes and troops will be ready to reach this planet soon. Our new starship could conducts planetary bombardment." Tagrin answered as he knows Maxter have been made captive.

Aloqi and his men report to Lorka on the information they fetch from the language interpreter device. The latter becomes worried and ordered many Zealseal pilots and Karploit crafts to patrol the atmosphere.

"Pilots, this is my order. Any unusual flying element from the space must be annihilated." Lorka ordered.

By dispersing more Zealseal pilots and craft to the moon, only a small number of Zarkano crafts would patrol around the landing zone. Next Lorka ordered the humans and the Pazarcar himself and his companions to be thrown into the cold prison.

"Look those Zarkano craft are patrolling the planet surface. But what can we do?" An American Jim Brown asked.

Aloqi reported to Zarkano that their fuel and energy system is running low as indicated on their instrument panel.

"We will extract rigourium from the sea water nearby to fill up our ships energy source." Lorka ordered as he inspect the human expedition force helicopters and an armored tank.

The Zarkano still use the eyzeme web to keep the guardians crew from awakening while each ships were connected by each type of energy pipe which is carried by the Zarkano remote energy channel. Next a large capital ship pull out a large crystal which connected to the sea below and the liquid substance begin to pull out from the ground through the energy absorber on the capital ship. The capital ship latches on the energy source by means of three tubes. The crystal is being protected by electro magnetic shield which was energized by capital ship power. Lorka's flagship and two other capital ships energy were replenished remotely from the capital ship which was connected to the crystal energy source. The Zarkano ground soldiers also used their portable energy gate device on the ground against any intruders. Then a shield of ten meters in height were energized around the base.

Meanwhile at the mountain, Commander Tagrin and the rest were devising a plan to rescue the humans. Commander Tagrin inspects the capture base surrounding from the range equipment and found it impossible to attack from the ground frontally.

"There are shields around the base. It is impossible to pass through without gaining the enemy attention and their numerical superiority would probably overcome us. The only way is to parachute across the tall shields during the turbulence of the sandstorm when the enemy cannot detect us and surprised them. But we do not have any plane or hang glider to flew us over." Commander Tagrin suggested.

"Any flying object will complete the job?Perhaps some alien birds here could grant us assistance." Johnny asked.

"I got an idea, we can draw some pictures on the paper and let that giant ape to identify where we can get those creatures. They may give us a clue." Lex answered.

The group agreed and they immediately seek out the ape to help them. When the apes arrive, Lex draws a large bird on a large white paper and shows it to the ape.

"Fly, you know like that." Lex said aloud as he flapped both his arms to simulate a bird movement.

A Russian and Jim Brown also demonstrate the flapping wings to the apes so as to recover some of the apes memory. Johnny and Commander Tagrin shows the drawn picture of a bird to apes.

The lead ape shake his head indicating a negative answer while flapping both his hand which leave much of the disappointment of the group. Suddenly he hold his both arm at ninety degrees and run around. The ape shakes his head indicating that an alien creature fly without flapping his arms.

"Fly like this." Lex asked again as the ape acknowledge again.

Later the ape point to the direction of his described flying creatures.

"He is hinting us to some location where we can find those birds. Let go there." Johnny shouted.

The group heads towards their direction and arrived at an open space one kilometer from the ape's resting area.

Meanwhile Lorka watched with amusement of the earth equipment such as the F-22 and notice its engine structure as compared with an helicopter and a transporter.

"It looks like they place their fuel system on different location which allows them to fly in different manner. But why did this large flying object with the same wing structure as this plane have such separated metallic objects as this flying objects." Lorka commented.

"Only those human can answered this. They looked more than a threat than those whom we encountered before. Once we are back in Carculand, they will suffered intensive interrogation for all information that we needed. Our capital ships energy are being replenished at the moment." Aloqi answered.

"Well done Aloqi. Indeed the humans have machinery that poised more menace to our ambition than those primitive beings. We will acquired knowledge on their capabilities and integrate their strongest element to improve our weakness. Looked at this vehicle, could this long tube be their weapon." Lorka speaks as he pointed to the tank.

Commander Tagrin and his group finally arrived and are amused at their findings.

"Five American World War two era planes. This is unbelievable. Somebody got us here before we do." Commander Tagrin asked.

"It could only be the missing five planes of the Flight 19. I learned from the coastal guards when I was a mechanic repairing planes." American Jim Brown answered.

"The Bermuda Triangle. I remember that the ambassador often mentioned about ships and planes mysteriously disappear across the Bahamas. So they have arrived here?" Lex answered.

"The only way to find out the truth is to inspect any diaries or log books in the vicinity." Commander Tagrin suggested.

"The plane number are FT-81 and FT-3. The others paintings had been defaced over a long period due to moisture but their wheels is also intact." Morrocan soldier Abdi Hamad replied.

The group dispersed and try to look out for clues in the area. Johnny found a bag hung on a tree and immediately search the belongings and found a diary and flip to the first page.

"Day 01 05 Dec 1945, we make a safe landing here after a futile search for the base. There are no a single soul around and the place is not even like Bahamas that we flew many times. We try to turn back a hundred and eighty degrees heads to our original search location but the compass is not working and points to the west. We notice the water is white and not the usual blue that we seen. After landing on the ground, we found the strange trees around which we never learn in our text books. Private Willy C."

"Day 02 06 Dec 1945, The daylight period on yesterday was longer than twenty hours before darkness appear. We try to contact base using our aircraft radio set but no to avail. Then we found ourselves in battle with strange large creatures. It was not any lion, tiger or crocodiles that we have seen. It was a large reptile with double inner teeth and it has fins on its top. I asked Lieutenant Flogan what is that,he gave me negative answers and told me that we could be in some lost island on earth. We studied the map and got on flight again. We try to search the landscape that could match our nearby countries. The land was so enormous, there is no soul. Worst of all when aerially inspecting the land formation it does not match the landscape or geographic patterns that could resemble any land on earth. Finally our fuel ran low and land in this area. Private Willy C."

Johnny flips to the last page of the diary to check for the fate of the crews.

"Day 320, Sergeant Tallyvan had died a month ago as a result of insufficient medical supplies caused by lethal poison of eating wild creatures thus leaving me alone. I shared the same symptoms as him and finding myself in state of dire and high perspiration. When somebody died I dig the grave for them. Several days ago I have predicted death will comes to me and my grave have been dug a few days ago. Tomorrow I will crept to my grave and face the sky till my time will come. Private Willy C."

Johnny looks around and finally found a skeleton on a half buried grave with the skeleton head looks to the sky. Johnny passed Tagrin the diary.

"They are your country men and the mysteries of this missing squadron are finally uncovered." Johnny speaks.

"Yes, now to the assembly point." Commander Tagrin suggested.

Comamnder Tagrin orders two American soldiers and a Japanese soldier to make a inspection of the old planes

"So how are we going to make a rescue attempt with such old planes and they do not have fuel." A Chinese soldier Pang asked.

"There is a way. A sand storm is arriving and we can used this as a cover. Next we can move these planes to the highest peak on this mountain and we are going to need the apes' help to make a bigger push. Then we will crash land over that shield and commenced the rescue operation. These old planes will not explode as it contains no volatile fuels inside and its heavy machine guns provided a fire power than our rifles." Commander Tagrin suggested.

"It is too risky, what if we died in the crash landing before any rescue attempt commences." A Moroccan asked.

"We can fasten our seat belts and hide our heads down in the cockpit before crash." An American Jim Brown suggested.

"A good suggestion. It is still the only way to make a rescue attempt. If we give up trying, we may end up like these dead pilots. Besides a sand storm could disrupt the enemy troops visibility." Johnny suggested.

"We have to sacrifice more chips to make the apes to help us." Lex suggested.

The group laughed and agreed. Lex draws the instruction of the picture and the apes finally help to tow the planes. Finally the sand storm arrives. Lex advised the apes to help them and it was successful.

Meanwhile in the prison base, Pazarcar air group and Maxter expedition team are locked up in the same room. The humans and the guardians are locked by an energy lock. Lorka pays a visit to Pazarcar.

"Hail Lord Pazarcar, today we shall be freed from your guardians atrocious demands over us." Lorka laughed.

"We never expected to breed such a dangerous nemesis. Our motive in this galaxy are creating a peaceful and united species." Pazarcar answered.

"Perhaps you misunderstood. The more highly advanced species will not treat others with dignity. They expect more from their return. I will demand the creation of life secrets as an addition to our demands for your release. Over the years, your shield was not improved and it led to the guardians demise when we released substance to negate your shield capabilities." Lorka requested.

"We have ourselves to blame for being self complacent. However there will be no way that I will give in your demands." Pazarcar asked.

"Give it a throughout thought before the Guardians Formation arrive to a fatal end." Lorka speaks as he left.

Aloqi arrived and informs Lorka that a sand storm will arrive soon who request the Karploit be withdrawn as they could suffer heavy damage and requires reprogrammed after collision. Lorka agreed and most of the Karploits are withdrawn to the capital ships. Commander Tagrin have observed how the Karploit opened and closed the entrance using the panel from their active screen.

Meanwhile the two apes started to throw the old planes to the air during the sand storm. The men hold tight during the somersault turn and fly like a paper plane. The team comprises of ten persons and five old planes: Commander Tagrin and American Captain Nigel Burns, Johnny and Lex, American Jim Brown and Abdi Hamad, Chinese Pang RuXi and Japanese Hiromi Yokosai, Briton George Baloke and Russian Sekoi Chvastki.

The Chinese and Japanese compliment each other.

"Both of our country bear hatred in the past, but today we are in the same team on a rescue mission. This is misery." Chinese Pang RuXi said.

"Yesterday war will only invoke painful memories. Today agenda is about saving earth. Our cooperation means saving more Chinese and Japanese lives. Forget the atrocities of the past and save the future." Japanese Hiromi Yokosai replied.

Finally the planes turn when it reached the base. The Karploits are shrouded by the storm and affect their visibility from detecting the planes. One of the Karploit is watching the sky and having no knowledge of the one of old planes piloted by Commander Tagrin splashed bullets on it which burst into flames when the heavy machine bullets pierced on the body. American Jim Brown and Hamad fired at the Zarkano guards and Karploits which is taken by suprises. One of the Zarkano guards laid dead and the two Karploits are blown up. Morrocan Abdi Hamad fired it with the rear machine gun and destroy a Karploit and destroy a shield generator which erupts several shield field destroyed. Both of them gets out and take over an anti aircraft gun which shot up much target. The Briton and the Russian shot up the unshielded Zarkano Zealseal and light Karploit craft and turn them to flames before landing. Johnny and Lex have to endure the sudden wind steep and turn its rudder, Lex fired on a eyzeme web in the air which have illuminated by the sands and destroys it. The sudden explosion pushed the plane to awkward position and smash towards the Karploit defences which stand guards on the transport destroying a few Karploits and they both let out of the plane. The Karploits chase towards them but commander Tagrin and Captain Nigel destroy them thus rescuing them. They run towards the base where Maxter was taken prisoners. The prison base are found to be shielded and Captain Nigel tries to hurl the grenades towards it but to no avail. The prisoners electronic lock is secured by the prisoners cell fuel system. It can only be unlocked when the fuel system is destroy which controls the electronic lock system.

The last plane flown by the Japanese and Chinese finds themselves head towards the base and Pang at the rear shot up unshielded light Karploit crafts parked near the prisoners base and exploded destroying the Karploits around.

"Pang, get ready to bail out. I need to conduct kamikaze against that shielded base, the light arms is useless. I will sacrifice myself to save humankind." Japanese Hirohmi requested.

"Hirohmi, please do not sacrifice yourself, there are other alternatives." Pang requested.

"A futile sacrifice could reverse the outcome in many disadvantage situation. Now go." Hirohmi urged.

Hirohmi's plane crashed onto base with Pang bailed out, shattering the shield and turn the plane upside down. A Zarkano guard fired at the plane and destroy it with a fiery explosion unwittingly because there is a torpedo hidden inside which was unknown to anybody. The explosion shattered the defences fuel system and fully remove the shields. Finally the cells are unlocked and the electronic locks on each person is released thus freeing the prisoners inside.

"Sir, the weather turns clear. But our planes are too far from here and the pilots could come across the heavy fire." Commander Tagrin asked.

"Take over that tent. I need to activate the guardians console which can provide shields for us. There are two Karploits which have a shield generator against our odds. Two fast penetrative shell could bring those down." Maxter ordered Commander Tagrin as the latter has manned an anti aircraft gun.

"Never mind, Jim Brown can take it down. Jim that robotics shield. Bring it down with consecutive two shots." Commander Tagrin ordered.

Jim Brown fired two an accurate shots which brings down the shield and a consecutive shots destroys the Karploits. Maxter races to the tent and uses the guardian console to activate the shields for the pilots and the soldiers.

Commander Tagrin and his men with the shield proceeded forward and they can fired through the shield and destroy many Karploits and killing Zarkano guards.

"It is fantastic and we can destroy them without loss." Vice Commander Rinco commented.

Finally the shielded group reached the air planes in the field. Maxter deactivated the shields from the console and allows the pilots, tankers and soldier to take up their tasks at their battle stations.

Chapter 8

Soon the jets fighters,offensive choppers drone and pilot manned planes are soaring in the skies. Commander Tagrin ordered all ground forces to protect the fighters against enemy forces. Even tanks joined the fight.

"What happens on the ground base?" Lorka asked.

"The humans break loose, we must send every crafts to destroy them and their flying machines." Aloqi asked.

"Activate the shield to protect the capital ships. Deploy only the Karploit crafts, I wanted to see those human machines performance against our Karploit crafts. Send more ZealSeal crafts to finish off the guardians' shuttle in the vicinity that they previously knocked off by our eyzeme web." Lorka asked.

The starship opened up a ledge and the light Karploit crafts came out in bunches. The choppers fired their first missile and engage a light craft. A light Karploit which being target by a guided missile was shredded by the latter when it hit the fuselage spot.

"Their ammunition could tracked our craft with awkward angle and destroy it easily unlike our extreme fixed targeting system. It is amazing. We must have such innovation." Lorka commented with amusement to Aloqi.

Meanwhile the experimental aircraft fired its high velocity gun on the large captial ships which is protected by the thick heavy shield and its shell was bounced off. The pilot was ordered to resume attack on other crafts.

"Those monstrous capital ships have heavy shields, our high velocity arsenal could not penetrate them." Maxter asked.

"The shields are very thick, they have overload energy beyond their fuel capacity. They must have an external fuel source feeding it. Request the console to locate their energy supply source." Pazarcar answered.

Maxter submit his mind wishes to the console and he found a energy source located near the sea and protected by a shield.

In the meanwhile the Zealseal pilots were trying to pick up the guardians target left in the ground. Senator Trulog's saucer was destroyed along with its crew after a few heavy hits from several ZealSeal beams.

"Those guardians saucer are even nut hard to crack after death." The ZealSeal pilots commented.

Pazarcar feel Senator Trulog's spirit speaking to him and he request help from Maxter to save more of the guardians.

"My alliance companions are being killed by the Zarkano pilots which they are stalked by the enemy lethal energy. We need to awake them so that this battle will not be lost. There are radiators which will nullify our shield capabilities, they must be wiped out." Pazarcar said.

"I will required the console to tell its location and translate the location to coordinates so that our planes can assist." Maxter answered as he translate his thought.

During the fight with the Karploit planes, the earth planes perform well to expectation. The new experiment chain gun fighter could penetrate the light Karploit craft shield from the front and destroy a few before disengage the fight. Meanwhile a drone fighter attacked a Karploits with its missile on the front, the shield is disable and the plane is throw out with its energy disruption and hits a speeding light Karploit craft which is destroyed. The latter craft also lose its shield due the impact it was destroyed by the vulcan canon of a F-22 who came in behind in the midst of recovering its energy. Another chopper tried very hard to evade a light Karploit craft and asked for help. American Jim Brown orders the ground anti aircraft crew to assist and they knocked off the light Karploit craft shields and sent it turning. While trying to recover, subsequent shot by the ground crew destroy it. Three Karploits crafts being ride by nine Karploits made an attempt to destroy the land forces from the ground. They met with a few Abrams tanks of the expedition and found their shots were bounced off the turret instead of penetrating as the latter are only vulnerable from the top with the Karploits weapons. Nevertheless perforated spots were left on the tank. The Karploits immediately report their inadequate shots to their ships. The three Karploits craft were subsequent shot up by the tank and left ablaze.

The F-15 and F-22 contains faster missiles which can penetrate the light Karploit craft in one shot. The energy ray of the light Karploit craft can be seen and the faster plane was able to evade the rays. Soon more of the light Karploit crafts are destroyed for loss of one choppers and a drone plane. The former was shot off the bladder and the ground crashed onto the river nearby but the crew is safe while the latter is shot up by the Karploit craft from behind.

Comamnder Tagrin ordered the fast plane to play roulette and allows the ground forces to engage the targets. This strategy will saved the planes ammunition and more pilots as well. A F-15 lured multiple Karploit crafts in fast speed while crews of American Jim Brown and Briton George Baloke engages them with large multiple ground anti aircraft fire which destroy large number of them.

"Those artificial Karploit crafts lack intelligence to detect their tricks and succumb to enemy coordinated ground forces fire. Now released the ZealSeal pilots." Lorka watched with shocked.

Maxter found the location of the energy crystal source and asked Commander Tagrin to destroy it.

"This energy crystal must be destroyed before they threatened the guardians or the battle is lost. It is located nearby and I need planes to go to this coordinates as the enemy planes are trying to wipe out the guardians' fleets. The radiators are a threat to the guardians, use the guided missiles or called upon the experiment plane to destroy it. They are always emitting electrical substances." Maxter suggested.

Commander Tagrin ordered that all the transport heavy plane have to be used to deliver missiles and supported the air and he dispenses order to the three F-22 to distort the enemy attention at the majority downed guardian fleet location. Next the pilots were issued orders to destroy all radiators than to combat the enemy craft.

Johnny meanwhile poured diesel into the old American Avenger plane which was part of the earlier rescue team.

"What are you doing?" Lex is amused and asked Johnny.

"Every bit of air effort counts and our planes might be deprived of ammunition fast." Johnny asked.

"But this plane has low velocity, more like a flying coffin I would say." Lex answered.

"I can navigate along the outer edge of the battle and occasionally ambushed on those enemy craft then turn back to the edge again. This will disrupt the enemy planes from hitting our planes. Our faster jets could intercept them as they are confused." Johnny answered.

"On the edge, I think you need someone to manned the rear gun to flank them from far away rather than risking this plane into the fields of beam." Lex answered.

"Great idea. In this case.." Johnny asked.

"I know, Let tucked in and fly." Lex answered and he brought two rocket propelled grenades along.

Johnny and Lex next flew the old avenger to the sky without any problem.

"It is flying after more than seventy years. It is truly amazing." Lex answered.

Next the Zealseal pilots from the capital ships begin to launch out, being heavy shielded they destroyed three drones and a chopper but they also lost one to guided missiles launched by a tornado at the rear of the engine. Eventually that Tornado was destroyed when two Zealseal craft cooperate in chasing it and destroying it. Subsequent Zealseal craft terrorized the ground and destroying several anti aircraft gun batteries. Tagrin ordered the ground air defenses missiles to be launched against ten incoming Zealseals craft. However the Zealseal pilots sway to the other side and destroyed a few rockets but one rocket exploded too near and causing one of the Zealseal craft shield to be dropped and and the pilot have to restart. The anti aircraft gun hits her and it drops to the ground but the pilot was safe. Next the Zealseal crafts initiate a rotating striking formation which the nine craft will turn a full circle which can avoid them getting hit in the rear engine. They destroyed many anti aircraft weapons in addition wounding and killing many soldiers, Maxter and Commander Tagrin runs for cover.

Three F-15 fired missile at the enemy formation and it scattered it with three enemy craft destroyed but two F-15 were lost when the Zealseals quick hovering allows them to engage the F-15 at the front. Next the missiles are launched again and catch three Zealseal unaware which felled to the ground with its shield gone. Next bombs are released from the jets and finally destroyed the Zealseal craft. However the remaining Zealseals managed to destroy another chopper and one Zealseal was brought to the the ground without shields and was destroyed by a tank driven by George Baloke and fired by Pang.

The earth pilots faces more danger and difficulty when Zealseal crafts enter the battle and more humans' planes were lost due to intelligence of the Zarkano pilot over the artifical intelligence Karploits who drive the Karploits light craft.

The avenger plane piloted by Johnny and Lex fight on the edge on the battle. Lex become frustrated when his rear gun shots fail to destroy any target, he shot a Karploit craft at the rear engine dropping its shield temporarily however a vulcan shot by a F-15 destroy it. Lex is disappointed and asked Johnny.

"I cannot downed any enemy with such junk gun. Can we get in closer?" Lex asked.

"No we are just lending support disrupting the enemies' concentration. It is a great aid to the struggling pilots out there." Johnny explained.

Lex continued with the shooting of the rear guns but cannot get gunned down any enemy, then he found a light Karploit craft is chasing a F-15. He take out a hand held rocket and fired on the the light Karploit craft which is traveling above the avenger. The rocket flew past the avenger which Johnny saw it strange and the light Karploit craft exploded and its debris shattered the cockpit of the Avenger and Lex finally celebrated. Johnny immediately turns the plane sideways and rotate it straight.

"What happened, I never saw such an airborne missile fired from our planes in this direction." Johnny asked.

"It is a hand held rocket fired by me. It is a good shot, isn't it." Lex replied.

"That is a silly attempt. You could get us killed. Are you trained to fire that rocket?" Johnny asked.

"No, we must use up every resources we have. Remember we save one pilot that could fight for another day. I still have one more here." Lex answered.

"Another one here! A small fragments of shrapnel hitting this plane could get us killed." Johnny asked with much surprise.

"Let see if I can get a good shot again. I would like to aim at those more powerful craft. Look the human base is being attacked. We could provide assistance." Lex answered.

"All right you can find some target with that. I will very appreciated that weapon will not found its target in this plane." Johnny speaks with a melancholic tone.

Finally one of the F-22 fired its missiles on the crystal but the shields block giving a bloating effects. He made a report to Commander Tagrin.

"Sir that crystal cannot be destroyed, the shields cover it." The pilot reported.

Maxter immediately find the console and try to activate to search for the crystal weak point using the costrolips. It provide the knowledge that the energy transfer at the weakest at the water which the Zarkano shield could not be activated at the water. Maxter feeds the information to Tagrin who ordered the pilot to make a low attack which could hit its vulnerable spots.

"Switch off the locking system, use the direct shot and launch from four hundred and eighty meters from the shield." Maxter ordered.

The F-22 pilot acknowledge the command and fired it, the missile loose heat as it touches the water and it hit twenty meters from the crystal vulnerability area. Sadly the crystal is still intact. The F-22 was destroyed when it was hit by multiple Karploits firing its beam from the shield stand.

"We lacked a torpedo that could travel inwards and blew that energy source apart." Commander Tagrin commented.

Meanwhile Lorka ordered more craft to protect the crystal shields.

The remaining three craft Zealseal attacked the ground forces as it the human have lost many anti aircraft guns. One of the drones fired at the one of the Zealseal craft and the latter lost its shield but managed to restore it. A Zealseal pilots intercepts a signal which controls the drones and fire at its drone control station killing the humans and all drones dropped from the sky. The transport firing its large missiles and the destroy the Zealseal craft, however it was attacked. The transport have its wings torn off and the fuselage blow up.

One of the remaining ZealSeal craft fired into the console area, killing three soldiers and damaging anti air battery. Commander Tagrin and Maxter evades the area but the metal tent crushes on the console and the latter tries to get it out. An Abrams tank driven by George Baloke and Captain Nigel destroy the Zealseal fighter with a close range tank shot by firing consecutively. Just when Captain Nigel was celebrating, they were fired aboard by the ZealSeal and the tank turret was gone. The pilot finds Maxter holding a console and turns the craft ready to fire at him. At this time Lex fired a hand held rocket from the avenger to the Zeal Seal craft who was destroyed at the engine and fell to the ground.

Maxter was surprised that World War two era planes had been brought from Earth on this journey and he speaks to Commander Tagrin.

"When was World War Two era planes made entry into our list of expedition forces." Maxter asked.

"No that was not, we found them stranded on this planet. They have been disappeared on the disputed Bermuda Triangle incident more nearly seventy years ago." Commander Tagrin answered.

Maxter recollects the details he had read up articles on the Flight 19 incident which occurs on the year 1945.

"The missing planes are torpedo bombers. These aircraft are capable to destroy the crystal energy source which the torpedoes can travel inwards the vulnerable area." Maxter suggested.

Commander Tagrin immediately radioed the avenger plane.

"Who are on that world war two junk plane?" Tagrin asked which is followed by Johnny affirmative answers.

"We need you to go the sea area and destroy the crystal energy source. Your plane possessed a weapon which could won us this battle." Tagrin commanded.

"How are we going to do?" Johnny asked.

Comamnder Tagrin pass the radio to Jim Brown who have experienced in repairing many planes at military air base.

"You will find a torpedo tube on your plane and you needed to move yourself to the middle cockpit and pull up the lever." The American Jim Brown explained.

Johnny informed Lex of their new mission.

"Commander Tagrin has a new mission for us. Move to the second cockpit. When you see the crystal energy, aim at the heart of crystal energy by using the periscope. Release the lever and we are home." Johnny said.

Lex obeys the order and he moves in the second cockpit. The Avenger middle cockpit was smashed by the debris earlier and it result in Lex easier to climb on to second cockpit. Commander Tagrin orders all planes to protect the avenger torpedo bomber.

Meanwhile four F-22 fired on the Zealseal with its missile who are destroying the guardians saucer. Two Zealseals were lost when they are burst on the rear engine by missiles. The F-22 then disperses the attention of the Zealseal craft and the Zealseal orders the F-22 decimation. A ZealSeal mades a sudden full hover to the side and surprise the F-22 with its beams killing the human pilot.

On the crystal energy source battle area, there are a lot furious battle going on as Lorka orders more craft to protect the crystals. Commander Tagrin order all the C-130 gunships, the experimental chain gun fighter plane, the helicopters and the remaining F-15, F-22,Tornadoes to make a counter attack around the crystal energy perimeter.

The gunships uses the side flank to defend by firing its chain gun, it proves successful as it shoot down the light Karploit crafts and Zealseal craft easily. However they are overwhelmed by the enemy and there are three only planes left. Two light Karploit crafts try to attack Johnny piloted Avenger but are destroyed by the experimental plane and a missile fired by the Apache chopper respectively. The Avenger finally arrived near the crystal energy source. They met Karploits being station on the top of the crystal shield, two F-15 fired their missiles and destroying large number of them, but the Zealseal destroy one F-15 by flanking on its side and trying to pursue the avenger. The Zealseal pilot was moving towards the avenger from the top angle, but Lex fired with its rear machine guns. The Zealseal craft was left undisturbed despite the hit but the spark from the machine guns distract the pilot visibility and he decided to hover to the avenger with high speed. However the A-378 experimental plane fired its last missile and knock the Zealseal off causing the shields to be down. The A-378 have expended its ammunition but the Zealseal pilot still tries to pursue the avenger with the shields down. The A-378 pilot decided to use the plane targeting self destruct system by targeting itself to the Zealseal craft.

"We must protect the old lady, co pilot eject the plane while I used the computer system to make a suicide attempt on that enemy craft." The pilot ordered.

The two pilots eject themselves after activating the plane computer system to make a suicide charge against the Zarkano

Zealseal craft which is successful and both of the planes are destroyed.

Johnny's Avenger finally arrived at the energy source and tweak his plane in to the vulnerable energy source. He fired the frontal fifty calibers machine on the wing, damaging the guarding Karploits. Next Lex released the torpedo by pulling the level. The torpedo dropped to the water and accelerates towards the crystal extraction vulnerable spot and the capital ships which connected its source to the crystal exploded due to the energy combustion reaction.

Finally Tagrin, Maxter rejoice over the successful attack. The eyzeme web was finally disabled due to the lack of energy and energy being use to curb the guardian beings' mind and physical mobility are finally removed.

In the fit of anger, Lorka ordered the launches of more craft and the capital ships begin to attack. The human ground forces fires their weapons in haste as the Capital ship of Lorka destroys three C-130 gunship after it repeatedly destroyed more than several light Karploit crafts with its cannon and two Zealseals with its heavy missiles. More human planes and its pilots were lost due to the large number of enemy beams which causing the planes harder to evade.

Pazarcar telepathically relate his messages to Maxter.

"We are still weak but we are free from the enemy influence energy. The console contains a security manipulation which it will demands the costrolips and your nerve axon in exchange, it can also allowed you to dedicated the costrolips in your body to save us to restore our energies. It could threaten your life. The numerous Zarkano forces will overwhelmed your forces very soon. Your people will be safe and so will be the galaxy." Pazarcar advised.

Maxter thus allowed the costrolips to be withdrawn so that its energy could be released to help the Guardians Formation which in turns threaten his life which the Guardians could not even repair. During the process, Maxter eyes and mouth releases several light sparks from his body. Finally all of the energy from Maxter's costrolips has been released. Pazarcar, Lacus and Calok finally restored their energy, they immediately activated their saucer remotely through their pisionic energies with their shield and protect the humans craft. Next all guardians in the downed saucer which have been incapacitated by the Zarkano eyzeme web begin to recover their mind and physical abilities.

"Those Zarkano scourges must eradicated completely with our full fledgling force. Relieve the beleaguered humans." Axerian urged.

Soon the survivors of the Guardian Formation fleet fully rises up and activate their shields. They destroys multiple Zarkano Zealseal crafts saving the three F-22 fighter planes. They rage towards the Zarkano and finally approaches the human base. Lorka capital ship begin to fled from the area when the massive Guardians saucers arrived.

The guardians' saucer eventually attacked the capital ships and other craft in the same sector. With the deactivation of the eyzeme web the Zarkano possess no weapons that could nullify the shields of the Guardians and many craft were destroyed as their eyzeme web were rendered inactive by the guardians in which they could not find power to activate those radiators again. Lorka ordered a full retreat to the space. However the guardians' fleet caught up with two large capital ships.

Ankoro's saucer which was previously captured is igniting its energy source with the living beings being awakened. It activated the electro magnetic shield and blew a large hole in its captor ship. It then destroys the fuel system of the captor ship uninterrupted and it ran aground. The other capital ship also try to escape from the guardians and its human allies after sustaining heavy hits. The Guardians saucer released its energy disrupting device and fired it accurately on the capital ships fuel line system. It handicap the ship movement and ran aground.

"The humans will be paid dearly for such insult. Now the truce is broken, we will occupied the planet of Roxan and pillage the resources till dry." Lorka ordered.

Pazarcar having seen Lorka capital ships retreated orders the conflict to be ended.

"Let them go, the humans will battle them in future. We must examined our losses." Pazarcar issued another command.

Finally the humans finally grounded all their remaining planes. Lex and Johnny immediately look for Maxter which is lying unconsciously at a tent.

"Johnny and Lex, you have brought the humans a great victory on its first pitched battle. Johnny your instincts bring credit to the human race." Maxter speaks.

"Rest well, Sir. Your foresight and bravery have brought the humans to a new age of unlimited advancement." Johnny replied.

The Guardians brings their console to treat the humans. Morrocan Abdi and Russian Severicus who lost a right arm and left leg respectively are being treated. They were brought to a transparent bed with liquid running the area. Axerian brought up a hologram and he released the liquid with the air gravity running. Next the human liquid of blood was flowed in and bones were grown. Abdi arm was regrown and Severicus leg was also reborn. Commander Tagrin was amazed by the advancement of the guardian in biological science.

"They make the impossible and soldier's amputated leg have been regenerate perfectly." Commander Tagrin commented.

"We hope we can have lesser human fatalities with their help." Vice Commander Rinco answered.

Pazarcar, Lacus and Ankoro examined Maxter and suggested he is impossible to be cured.

"The duration for his costrolips to purge out has passed and its main liquid was used to save us as it cannot be exchanged with the console. The remnants of the secondary costrolips will severe every blood veins which is not possible to remove. It will impregnated another blood cells and spread in a quick manner. Only our creators could find solution to this." Ankoro speaks.

"We respect your explanation. He saves us by sacrificing himself. We ought to compensate the human beings pact with more favors. It is our honor towards him." Pazarcar agreed as he turns to Maxter.

"The costrolips is our creator's mystery. We are unable to cure you. The human pact will be repaid accordingly. It is our best compensation. Spend your last moment with your friends and pick a nominee for your post. We fail to make new progress for our offensive and defensive capabilities which causes us to land in such bad situations. However your sacrifice helped to turn the tide against them." Pazarcar speaks to Maxter.

"Having new powerful weapons will transformed the guardians' agenda to dominate rather than cultivate peaceful evolution. I have a nominee for my post." Maxter turns to Johnny.

"Johnny, you have compensate my wrongdoings of curiosity that costs lots of human being lives. I will like you to be the new Ambassador to the guardian formation." Maxter asked.

"I felt obliged to took up such responsibilities, I afraid that I cannot perform the task to expectation." Johnny answered.

"Johnny, the human race need to carry on its goal. Without it, the humans are heading towards slow extinction in our own solar system." Maxter says.

"Alright, I will take over the post for the time being till a better man emerged. Your sacrifice have rehabilitated your deeds. You will rank among the great historic men. Rest in peace." Johnny agreed.

"Thanks for your help. I understand your heavy responsibility. Do take care of Lex." Maxter speaks his last words as he passed away.

Pazarcar, Ankoro and Axerian uses the hologram to scan Johnny brain waves and found him satisfactory for the post.

"Your human destiny lies with you. You are the only one who will communicate with us on our treaty. Honor on your predecessor legacy and continue to lead your race well." Pazarcar speaks.

"I will continue his legacy. First we need to get back to earth and forging a proper plan. Commander Tagrin, fixed all planes. We are going home and coming back here stronger.

The Zarkano prisoners will be in your custody till we return back and conceived a plan for these prisoners. We will enact a truce with the Zarkano for the prisoners of war protocol so that the prisoners will not suffer savages and brutal treatment." Johnny requests.

"I agreed. They are your pawns and the war belong to you. The Zarkano have discovered weakness in our defensive capabilities and we need to examine our deficiencies. We will aid you behind the battle however. " Pazarcar replied.

The next day, the guardians sent the earth expedition force back to earth. The alliance created a vacuum tube which the humans could travel safe without any deadly hazard which the planes passed through previously.

Johnny finally arrives on Earth and he delivered a speech on many forms of media where many people in every country are watching.

"Dear earthlings I am Johnny Carlson. From the complicated debut victory battles over the Zarkano the aggressive species of the star system the humans have gain a foothold in the a new Star System. We have made a new agreement with the Guardian Formation of the Syfelium Star System. The humans will receive greater treatments from the them. First, the humans are free to colonize any inhabitant land not occupied by intelligent species. In the second treatment, electro-magnetic shield technology will receive reverse engineering for the humans with the greatest assistance by the guardians. On the third exchange, they will help us on the fossil fuels fast reproduction with the creation of large animals being breed on earth. We need vast fuel to overcome the Zarkano. In addition the human are treated to additional gifts. The first gift, the Guardian Formation will educated earth scientist in the creation of the portal between earth and the planet Altro.

However till the first completion of the human made portal, the Guardians have provided us a portal to the star system and we will fully handled our transportation. The second additional gift is they will work with us to construct large armed starships so that the decisive battles with the Zarkano will turn out in our favor. We must continue such upheaval tasks till when the battle reaches Carculand, the Zarkano home planet or the enemy will finally consider for an armistice in the new solar system. Till then sacrifices will be inevitable, but the humanity's future reveal a great radiant light ahead."

Finally Johnny inhaled his breath and prepare for a final speech.

"Humanity interstellar success should be attributed to valiant efforts and sacrifice of the former earth ambassador, Mister Maxter. We will not never forget his greatest contribution to mankind and will always be honored forever."

Johnny's speech end with the portrait of Maxter being broadcast in the news. The politicians rising from their seats paying homage to Maxter after a salute by soldiers.